"I've heard Central Park is quite dangerous at night," I said.

"Are you forgetting you're with a cop?" Carl asked. "This is not a water pistol on my hip, pardner."

"Lead on, sheriff," I said.

As we walked, I noticed how easily we matched pace. Carl is tall for a Japanese, I'd say about five-ten. I'm just five-four. But there was no disparity in our gait. He has an easy, graceful way of moving that makes you feel comfortable. We chatted along the way, and I'm afraid it was mostly about me. He did seem genuinely interested. By the time we'd reached the Plaza, he knew most of what there is to know about me. And, I'm ashamed to say, I knew very little about him, save that he was fun, handsome, and easy to be with. On short acquaintance, a person really doesn't need much more.

"Sheer entertainment with a light touch of romance in an amusing suspense story that will have wide appeal." —*Booklist*

"A grand finale on the George Washington Bridge caps this breathless thriller." —*School Library Journal*

". . . an unusually appealing heroine."
—*The Horn Book*

Other books in this series
Doris Fein: Quartz Boyar

Also available from
VAGABOND BOOKS

Blackbriar
  by William Sleator
Girl Meets Boy
  by Hila Colman
The Forever Formula
  by Frank Bonham
Fours Crossing
  by Nancy Garden
Seven Days to a Brand-New Me
  by Ellen Conford

DORIS FEIN SUPERSPY

by
T. Ernesto Bethancourt

Vagabond Books

SCHOLASTIC BOOK SERVICES
New York Toronto London Auckland Sydney Tokyo

For all the loyal Americans who endured,
1942–1945

ISBN 0-590-32382-2

Copyright © 1980 by Tom Paisley. All rights reserved. This edition published by Scholastic Book Services, a division of Scholastic Inc., 50 West 44th St., New York, NY 10036, by arrangement with Holiday House, Inc.

12 11 10 9 8 7 6 5 4 3 2 1   6   2 3 4 5 6 7/8

Printed in the U.S.A.   01

Contents

1/New York, N.Y.   page 1
2/I Meet a Detective   page 15
3/Trouble in Dakama   page 32
4/At the UN   page 45
5/Kidnapped!   page 56
6/Not So Secret Agents   page 71
7/Enter: Harry and Larry   page 89
8/The Prisoner of the Hilton   page 104
9/Embarrassed at the Bridge   page 117
10/Paris in the Spring?   page 128

1

New York, N.Y.

"We are now approaching Kennedy Airport," the flight attendant's voice said over the intercom. "Please extinguish smoking materials, fasten your seat belts and see that seats and seat trays are in an upright position."

I looked out the window, and there it was. The New York skyline. It was almost 1:45 P.M., and though the lights in the skyscrapers weren't yet visible, it was still impressive. The big jet angled away then, and I was treated to a view somewhat less thrilling. A sprawl of smaller buildings and a pall of yellowish smog. But I suppose it isn't called smog in New York. Maybe New Yorkers don't know it's there, or simply ignore it. They seem to have a talent for ignoring things in New York.

But it was thrilling. I always wanted to see New York, and now I had my chance. The trip was my reward for finishing at the top of my class at Santa Amelia High, in my home town of Santa Amelia in Southern California. It was also my first air trip cross-country. Up to now, I'd never been farther east than Las Vegas. And that was because my dad was attending a medical convention there. Mom and I went along. They say Las Vegas is the most exciting city in the west. I found it a bore.

I don't gamble, and being something of a feminist, the idea of seeing a girlie show leaves me cold. I must also admit that having had a teensy weight problem all my life, the shows would have been doubly depressing. But I did see Tom Smith, the Welsh heartthrob for middle-aged ladies. His act was almost completely macho-sexist and filled with cutesie-poo double meanings. About the time some women my mother's age began throwing their hotel room keys onto the stage, I walked out.

But New York! This would be different, I thought. There was the Museum of Modern Art, the Metropolitan, Lincoln Center, Carnegie Hall, the theater district. I was excited, and frankly, I don't think any person in the world could *not* be. I'd been reading about this city and hearing about it for most of my life.

I had a good idea of where things were located. When I first found out I'd be visiting my aunt and uncle, I sent away for all the city maps, brochures and fliers I could. And I'd been studying them for weeks. For instance, my aunt Lois (she's my mother's sister) and my uncle Claude (he's with the UN) live on East 79th Street. That would be just blocks from the Metropolitan Museum of Art and the Guggenheim. The UN is thirty-five blocks farther south. To

2

get there, one may take a taxi, a bus, or the subway. I even had a complete map of the New York City transit system in my bag. In my insularity, I thought then I was ready for anything New York could hand out. I should have known better.

Just hours before, when Larry Small saw me off at Los Angeles International Airport, I positively exuded confidence.

"Dee," he'd said, "are you sure it's gonna be all right? I mean, your leaving a day early and all?"

"I sent a telegram to my aunt and uncle letting them know, Larry," I replied. "And there's no need for anyone to meet me at the airport. If I can't take a cab from Kennedy to their apartment in Manhattan, I shouldn't be allowed out after dark."

"That's another thing," Larry said. "That place is dangerous. I've read about the things that go on in New York. And it's scary, Dee."

"Don't be foolish, Larry," I said. "Scary things go on everyplace. After all, didn't we have a murder and another one attempted just months ago? Right here in Santa Amelia?"

Larry had to admit I was right. In fact, you may have seen the story on TV or read about it in the papers. There was an attempt on the life of Danny Breckinridge, the rock singer. He bills himself as *Dr. Doom,* lately. A half-crazed kid, Arnold Whitman, fired a rifle at Breckinridge from the light booth during a rock concert at the Santa Amelia Civic Auditorium. The bullet missed Breckinridge, but hit and killed Danny's bass player. And that wasn't half of it.

It seemed that everyone involved had something to hide, and I must say that I played a key part in unraveling the mystery. In the process, I got to know

Danny Breckinridge fairly well. I'm not name-dropping, mind you. Simply stating facts. But that's another story. I should explain about Larry Small though.

You could say that Larry and I have an understanding. It just may be that we've known each other for so long that we drifted into a relationship. Larry's mother and mine went to nursing school together. Almost from the day that his parents were divorced, and Larry and his mother moved back to Santa Amelia, our parents have been throwing us at each other. And since the Danny Breckinridge affair, we've become quite close.

Larry was editor of our high school paper, *The Blade,* and I was number one reporter. I suppose that I could have been editor myself, but Larry had been on the *Blade* staff longer than I, and got the job through seniority. But not without ability or talent. He's really quite bright, in an unapplied way. All he's ever been interested in is rock music and writing about it. His knowledge of the field verges on the encyclopedic, and his writing style is very engaging, in a *Rolling Stone* fashion.

But Larry got so wrapped up in his extracurricular journalism that he almost didn't graduate. I helped him as much as I could, and he barely squeaked by. Just now, he's writing a novel, a *roman à clef,* about the Breckinridge murder attempt. While he's doing that, he's working as a copy person and cub reporter on the *Santa Amelia Register.* The editor in chief, Dave Rose, gave him the job after graduation.

Larry's become quite possessive of me lately though. And when he learned about my vacation in New York City, he was concerned that some horrible

4

fate would befall me in the Big Evil City. Charming, in its own way, but claustrophobia-making on occasion. Especially when I told him that I was leaving a day sooner than I'd planned.

Mom and Dad had already left for their vacation, in Hawaii. It was part of another professional junket for Dad, and the date was firm ages ago. I saw them off at the airport just two days before I was due to leave for New York.

Once they'd gone, I realized that I'd already said my good-byes to everyone and would be sitting around Santa Amelia for an extra day before my aunt and uncle expected me in New York. I was so excited about the trip, I decided not to wait. I mean, it was so *anticlimatic,* having to wait out another day in Santa Amelia. I sent a telegram to my aunt and uncle saying I was arriving a day early, and not to bother meeting me at the airport. I'd arrive at their place the next afternoon. And Larry was concerned.

"What if they're not home, Dee?" he asked. "Where will you go? Where will you stay?"

"Larry, Larry," I replied, "they have this marvelous new invention. It's called a hotel. I have plenty of cash and traveler's checks. If Aunt Lois and Uncle Claude are away, I'll check into a hotel until they return. In fact, it would be nice to stay at the Plaza. I've wanted to see it ever since I read *Eloise,* years ago when I was small."

Then of course, I had to explain to Larry that *Eloise* is a children's book about a little girl who lives at the Plaza Hotel. Larry can tell you how many hairs the singer Bruce Springsteen has on his chest, but his literary background is a bit spotty.

"All the same, Dee," he'd said, "you will be careful, won't you? You mean a lot to me." It sounded so sweet that I kissed him. Just then, the flight began boarding. I can still see him, standing there at the gate, looking worried. But all I felt was eagerness to see New York. As I sat on the plane, awaiting take-off, I said to myself, "Well, here goes Doris Fein, world traveler!"

The passengers on the plane fell quiet now. That sort of electric silence air travelers fall into on take-offs and landings. It wasn't until the wheels chirped on the landing strip and the jet engines reversed that conversation resumed and the tension eased.

"Ladies and gentlemen," the flight attendant said over the intercom, "we have just landed at Kennedy International Airport in New York. The temperature is 76 degrees Fahrenheit, 24 degrees Celsius, and Eastern Daylight Time is 1:45 P.M. We hope you had a pleasant flight and that we will see you soon again on Pan Am Airlines. Have a nice day in New York."

I had to laugh. I'm so sick of that *have a nice day* line. It's said so often that it has no meaning. I can't help but imagine some scene in, say, a social-service agency, where this desperate man comes in for help and encounters a career civil servant.

MAN: You've got to help me. I have no money, no job. I haven't earned a cent in six months. My children are starving, I have teeth so bad they're falling out. My wife is growing another head in the middle of her chest, and we're being thrown out on the street!

CLERK: Sorry, sir. From your file here, you have no benefits entitlement. We can't help you.

MAN: Then I'm leaving here, and I'm going to shoot myself! (He turns to leave)

CLERK: (Calling after him) Have a nice day!

You see what I mean? I accepted my *have a nice day* again from the stewardess at the plane exit. I wondered absently if airline stews have more teeth than ordinary women, or if it's just that they somehow are able to show them all when they smile.

Kennedy Airport didn't look all that different from Los Angeles International. Dad says that if there weren't names on them, you'd never know what city you were in from the airports. They all seem the same. But the people were sure different.

In the space of time it took me to get to baggage claims, I heard conversations in Spanish, French, Italian and some languages I couldn't recognize. And the people themselves! Black, tan, Oriental, Hispanic . . . I even saw a man in a turban!

That may not sound so noteworthy to you if you live in a cosmopolitan area. But I'm from a small city in Southern California. In Santa Amelia, it sometimes seems that all the girls are blond, blue-eyed and willowy thin. The guys often look the same, but with longer hair. If I weren't an avid reader with an itch to travel, I might have lived out my life in Santa Amelia thinking that everyone was supposed to look like Barbie and Ken. And as my hair is mousy brown and I've worn dresses out of Ladies' sizes since I was thirteen, it did tend to hammer down my self-esteem a bit.

But I do have clear skin that draws compliments, and because my uncle Saul is a dentist, I promise you that my teeth are perfect. My eyes are green, and my

7

lashes are long. I guess my eyes and teeth are my best features. Funny, I read not long ago that when Raquel Welch was asked what she felt was her best features, she said her teeth! Me and Raquel.

After waiting longer for my baggage than it takes to fly from Chicago to New York, I finally got through baggage claims and to an exit marked: *To Taxis*. There was a line of cabs waiting. In fact, there were more cabs in that line than there are in all of Santa Amelia. Of course, there being only six cabs in Santa Amelia, that's not saying much.

I waved at a cabbie, and he roared up to the head of the line so fast I had to step back, for fear he'd be unable to stop in time. My mistake. When I stepped back, a businessman-type with an attaché case and a golf bag darted in front of me and into the cab before I could move! By the time I'd collected my wits, my cab was disappearing with Mr. Polite in the back.

Now, I don't approve of all this light-the-cigarette, open-the-door, and pay-the-check-in-restaurants crap. It's positively medieval. But there *is* such a thing as common courtesy, person-to-person. While I was reflecting on this, I'll be darned if it didn't happen to me again! The next cab in line roared up, and this time I was faked out by a little old woman, straight out of a *New Yorker* cartoon. She elbowed me in the ribs when she stole my cab, too!

I learn quickly. When the next cab pulled up, I stood firm as a toreador before a bull. By the time he had stopped rolling, I had my hand on the door handle and in a new land-speed record try, I hurled my suitcase, flight bag, and garment bag in back. I almost leaped in after my luggage!

"Eight-twenty East 79th Street, driver," I said. Then I looked around me at the cab's interior. I felt like I was in jail. There was an armored partition between me and the driver, with a change drawer in back of the driver's seat. The upper part of the partition seemed to be made of bulletproof glass. Evidently, New York cabbies are ripped off at an alarming rate and such things are necessary. But I felt like I was riding shotgun on a Wells Fargo stagecoach.

The interior of the cab was filthy, and there hung in the air a miasma made up of equal parts stale cigars and unwashed humanity. As the driver pulled away from the cab stand and the air began to flow through the vent holes in the glass partition, I soon discovered that most of the aroma was emanating from my driver! I opened a side window and, as unobtrusively as possible, sat in the stream of muggy air that came through.

The driver made an entrance onto a freeway marked Van Wyck Expressway in a maneuver best described as *kamikaze* cabbie. It was the last bit of fast driving I saw on that trip into Manhattan. I don't know if I had arrived in the teeth of some sort of mid-afternoon rush, or if traffic is that way all the time in New York. The freeway, or the expressway, as they call it in New York, was a parking lot. One hour and twenty dollars later, I was standing in front of the high-rise apartment house where my aunt and uncle live. I was beginning to think that the rest of my vacation would be spent in that smelly cab. The doorman opened the cab door, and I told him, "I'm visiting the Bernards. Apartment 16-D."

I gave my aunt's married name with the French pronunciation: Bear-NAHR. The doorman gave me a blank look, then his face lit up.

"Oh, you mean the BOIN-ards," he said. "Yeah, they're in 16-D." I should have realized. Uncle Claude is with the UN delegation from the African republic of Dakama. Dakama used to be a French colony, but they gained autonomy years ago. Uncle Claude's family had lived in Dakama for generations, and he was born there. Just now, the government is in the process of converting to black rule. But many of their officials are native-born whites. Uncle Claude, for instance. He still has an important post because he was among the few that pushed for black Dakamans in government. I understand from Mom that his family is extremely wealthy and his concern wasn't for the family holdings in Dakama, which are only a small part of their wealth, but in human rights.

But Uncle Claude speaks French. Or I should say that he grew up speaking French. He speaks English, Dakaman, Swahili, Japanese and German, too. I was looking forward to meeting him. All I'd seen were pictures of him and Aunt Lois together. Judging from the snapshots, he's about six feet tall, with a well-trimmed beard; dark haired and *verry* handsome. Of course the only snaps I'd seen were years and years old. From when he and Aunt Lois were first married.

I stood in front of the apartment door marked 16-D and rehearsed my speech. If Uncle Claude came to the door, I was going to say, *"Bonjour, Oncle Claude. Je suis Doris Fein, votre nièce."* I rang the bell and almost immediately, the door opened. I was face to face with a man in his early forties. He didn't have a beard, though. He was the same size and coloring as the pictures I'd seen of Uncle Claude. And he *could* have shaved his beard. Men change their appearances so much with facial hair. Dad had a mustache for years when I was little. Mom says when he shaved it off, I cried and didn't recognize him. So, I gave the man in the doorway my little speech in French. I got a blank look from him for easily five seconds. Understandable, I suppose. We'd never met. Then he smiled a ravishingly charming smile and said in French, "My dear niece, how charming! And what a wonderful surprise!"

He embraced me in French family style, kissing me on both cheeks. Then we both said, in English, at the same instant, "Didn't you get my telegram?" We both laughed. And when we stopped laughing, we both tried to talk at the same time again. He finally held up a hand.

"Attendez!" he smiled. "Perhaps we should begin anew? I sent a wire to you this morning. I have been recalled to Dakama. I must leave with your aunt at once. There are governmental troubles at home that only I can resolve." He saw the look on my face. I must have appeared crushed. And rightly so. I'd been looking forward to this trip so. "But don't fret, *mon petite chou,"* he said. "We shan't be gone for long. In the meantime, we shall arrange accommodations for you."

"But what about here?" I asked.

Uncle Claude's face darkened. *"Impossible,* I'm afraid," he said sadly. "This apartment is not ours. It belongs to the Dakaman legation to the UN. A group of diplomats will be staying here. I will make arrangements for you to stay at a hotel. Would you prefer the Hilton or the Plaza?"

11

"The Plaza," I said, abstractedly. This was all going so fast.

"Très bien," said Uncle Claude. "The Plaza it shall be."

"Where's Aunt Lois?" I asked. Uncle Claude looked evasive.

"She's doing some last minute shopping, I'm afraid," he said. "When she learned we were going home to Dakama, she remembered all her promises to pick up things for friends at home. Especially for her women friends. Dakama City is hardly Paris, you know."

I didn't know, but I nodded, knowingly. Uncle Claude assumed I was more worldly and traveled than I was. I didn't want to disabuse him of the idea. I also didn't want him to get the opinion that I was a hopeless hick from California. He might have put me on the next plane back to L. A. And I wasn't going to be denied my New York vacation!

"I must make arrangements at the hotel," Uncle Claude said. "Excuse me, please." He showed me into the living room, while he went into another room to telephone.

The apartment was gorgeous. It was furnished in Scandinavian style, all chrome, white upholstery, rosewood, and teak. It took me a while to realize that the Klee, Dufy and Buffet oils on the walls weren't reproductions at all, but originals! The floors were brilliantly polished parquetry with Rya rugs that would have cost Daddy half a year's work. After about ten minutes, Uncle Claude came back into the living room.

"Doris," he said, pronouncing it *Doh-ree,* which I liked, "I have made all the arrangements. You will be in Suite 812 at the Plaza. I've also called the department stores we patronize, and have drafted a letter of permission to use our accounts. Use them freely. You only need identify yourself. I presume you have a California driver's license?"

"Oh, yes, Uncle," I said, my head spinning. "I even have my passport." I caught his look of inquiry. "In case I ever go anywhere, that is," I said, smiling.

He laughed and said, *"Bon!* I can see you are a very independent young woman, Doree. I only hope you can forgive us for this inhospitable situation, but it *is* a matter of state. And now, I must go down to the UN building. Forgive me. I'll see that your bags are brought to the Plaza. Why don't you see some of the sights; do some shopping. By the time you are finished, your suite will be prepared for you." He glanced at his watch. I could see it was a Patek-Philippe. "Your aunt and I will meet you for dinner in the Oak Room at . . . nine o'clock. Then we must take a midnight flight to Dakama. Will that be agreeable?"

"I . . . guess so . . ."

"Good! Then it is all arranged," he said, giving me a dazzling smile. His teeth were excellent. "Now, let me see you to a cab."

Before I could say another word, he had me by the elbow and was guiding me down the hall to an elevator. In the lobby, he had the doorman hail a cab for me. While the doorman was out in the street whistling for a taxi, he handed me a piece of paper.

"Here is a list of the stores where we have accounts," he said. "Do you know how to get to them?"

"I have a map," I said.

He gave me another double kiss, and put me in the

13

waiting cab. Then he quickly went back into 820 East 79th Street. I realized that the driver was looking askance at me.

"Where to, girlie?" he asked.

I glanced at the list of stores and caught my breath. Then in my best imperious fashion I ordered, "Saks Fifth Avenue, please!"

2

I Meet a Detective

I'd be lying if I said that I didn't enjoy seeing the stores. And naturally, I didn't charge anything to my aunt and uncle's accounts. It was enough to know that I could, had I wanted to. I'm not one of those people who can shop without a purpose or without the money to make a purchase. But somehow, knowing that I *can* buy removes the necessity to spend the money. I don't know if that makes a bit of sense, but that's the way I am.

Saks Fifth Avenue was great fun. I saw clothes actually made for women my size that didn't look like little old lady styles! And the accessories, lingerie, and jewelry! I felt as though I was a kid in a candy store. One that the kid's father owned. And after Saks came Bergdorf's, to show me that Saks' prices weren't all that high by comparison. But when I hit Bloomingdale's, I fell in love. The place seems to be geared to young adult taste in almost every department. I promised myself that if I ever lived in New York City, it would be my one charge account. It's a real department store, and you could furnish yourself and your apartment from start to finish there. As to the gourmet groceries and cheese departments, I won't comment but to say that I could gain weight just on the aromas!

Yet, for all the fun I was having, I kept getting this feeling of a subtle *wrongness* somewhere. And I swear I was being followed. Which of course, I was. Unless you've seen the crush of humanity that comprises an average day in New York City, you mightn't understand. There is simply no place you can go alone except for a stall in a restroom. There's alway someone behind you. But this feeling was different. It was that prickly-back-of-the-neck sensation you get when someone is reading over your shoulder. I turned abruptly a few times to look behind me. Each time I did, I saw scads of people. I don't know what I expected to see, anyway.

Instead of a cab from Bloomie's, I walked over to Fifth Avenue and to the Plaza Hotel. Walking three blocks in New York is like seeing a show. In the short walk to the Plaza, I saw enough sights, human and architectural, to fill a short lifetime.

The Plaza was straight out of the pages of *Eloise*. I wasn't disappointed in any aspect of it. The lobby, the shops, the restaurants . . . I half expected to see Eloise with her pet turtle, pouring water down a mail chute.

I had no trouble at the desk. My suite was ready for me, and a bellperson showed me to my floor.

Magnificent! I had a view of Central Park that was panoramic, and my bags were already in the room when I got there. I tipped the bellperson a quarter and got a look from him that would have withered an Eskimo. I made a mental note to get a bunch of single dollar bills for future tips at this place. When you drop a quarter into a waiting palm at the Plaza, it's as though you'd spit in it instead of tipped!

I busied myself for a while with unpacking, and after I was done, the jet lag hit me. It was close to eight o'clock and all during my shopping tour, I hadn't eaten a bite. Virtue may have its own reward, but all I had was a feeling of weakness, verging on nausea. Petunia was at it. Petunia is my alter ego, the one that can't pass a Baskin-Robbins ice cream store, and the person for whom a Big Mac attack is a chronic disease. I glanced at my watch. If I could sit on Petunia for an hour, I'd make it until I joined Aunt Lois and Uncle Claude for dinner downstairs in the Oak Room.

To show you how virtuous I was, I only scanned the room service menu twice before I changed for dinner. True, I was at a table in the restaurant by ten to nine, but punctuality is a virtue, too.

By nine-thirty, with Aunt Lois and Uncle Claude a half hour late, I had consumed a full basket of small rolls and bread sticks with gobs of butter. When my waiter refilled it, I could hear Petunia grunt in triumph! I'd made serious inroads into the second bread basket when my waiter returned and handed me an envelope addressed to me in a flowing script. When I turned it over to open it, I saw my aunt's name engraved on the back flap.

Dear Doris,

So very sorry we won't be able to have dinner to-gether. Things have worsened at home in Dakama, and we had to leave earlier than planned. I'm deso-late we couldn't get together, but Claude's duty to my adopted country comes first and foremost. It's one of the hazards of la vie diplomatique. Do enjoy your stay at the Plaza, and I hope so very much that we'll be back in a few days. We'll see the sights and some shows then. Forgive me for stranding you this way.

> *Love,*
> *Aunt Lois.*

I got a return of the chills I'd felt earlier on my shopping tour. The being-followed feeling was noth-ing compared to this. I've been receiving letters and cards from Aunt Lois ever since I can remember. I know her handwriting as well as my own. Which is understandable, as Mom, Aunt Lois and I are all left-handed. This letter was written by a right-handed person! There was no mistaking the right-hand tilt to the script. I suppose a right-handed person wouldn't have noticed such a thing, but anyone who has struggled through life with packages that open the wrong way, typewriters, can openers, automobiles and, well, nearly everything you can name being geared to a right-handed world would spot it in a flash.

I sat there at the table, and the half-eaten roll in my mouth turned to ashes. Even Petunia stopped growling. There was something terribly wrong going on, and I didn't know what it was, or what to do about it! I sat there in a brown study for another half hour. Finally, I decided what to do. I would get in touch with the police.

Having made my decision, and at Petunia's urging, I had a Caesar Salad with a carafe of Chablis. I had a task before me, and there was no sense in not keeping up my strength.

* * *

"Lookit, lady, I'm sorry," said the detective at the 141st Precinct, "but this don't even come under the jurisdiction of the New York City Police Department. Your relatives are UN people."

It had taken me nearly an hour of persistence to get past a desk sergeant downstairs and upstairs to the detective squad room. I wasn't about to be put off.

"But there's something wrong, dreadfully wrong, going on!" I insisted.

The detective, whose name was Linderman, according to the plaque on his desk, sighed deeply and looked around the crowded, dirty office. There were two other detectives sitting at desks. One, a middle-aged man, and the other, a young Oriental. "What am I supposed to do?" asked Linderman. Neither of the other men so much as glanced up.

"Listen, girlie . . . " he began.

"Ms. Fein," I corrected.

"Okay, okay, Ms. Fein, then. Let's just backtrack one more time. Now your relatives are with the UN, right?"

"Correct."

"And they are foreign nationals as well as diplomatic corps, right?"

"My uncle is, my aunt was born in California."

"Whatever. She's married to your uncle, ain't she?"

"Of course she is."

"Then don't you see?" said Linderman. "They're outa my jurisdiction. I couldn't even write a parking ticket for your uncle. He could light a cigar with it, if he wants to."

"I'm not talking about a parking ticket," I said firmly. "I'm talking about possible foul play. Maybe they've even been kidnapped or something!"

"Even so, that's a Federal offense, kidnapping. And you ain't got a shred of evidence that anything's wrong."

"They're missing, I tell you."

"They are like hell," said Linderman, angrily. "You got a note on your aunt's stationery telling you where they went."

"That is not my aunt's handwriting," I said, indicating the letter that Linderman was holding. "It's her stationery, but she didn't write that."

"Looka here," said Linderman, "are you a graphologist, girl — uh, Ms. Fein?"

"No."

"Well, there you are. You could be wrong."

"But I'm not," I persisted. "That note was written by a right-handed person. My aunt is left-handed, like I am."

"But you're not a handwriting expert, are you?" snapped Linderman. "You just do like it says in the letter. Enjoy your stay at the Plaza. You want to make sure nothing's wrong, call the UN and confirm that your uncle's in Ichama . . . "

*"Da*kama," I corrected. "And it's too late. Their office hours are over and tomorrow is Sunday. I've already called, before I came here, and all I get is an answering machine with a message in Dakaman and French."

"Then there's nothing more to do, is there?" asked Linderman, with supreme illogic. "Go home, or to your hotel and get some sleep. Take Sunday off. I wish I could. Go to St. Patrick's and say a prayer. It'll do just as much good as I can."

"I'm Jewish."

"Then go to Temple Emanu-El!" he growled. "Go anywhere but my squad room! It's outside my jurisdiction, I tell you!"

"I heard you," I said, getting up. "May I have my letter back?"

"Here, here," he said. "And you wait and see. When you call the UN on Monday, they'll tell you what I did. There isn't a thing wrong!" Linderman busied himself with some papers on his desk.

I knew there was no point in trying to convince him any further. I put the letter in my bag and started for the door. As I passed the desk where the young Oriental detective was seated, he tapped me on the arm. Startled, I looked askance at him.

"Listen Ms. Fein," he said in a heavy New York accent, "I think you may be on to something." He reached into his wallet and handed me his card. It read *Detective Carl Suzuki, New York Police Department.* "I'm about to go off duty. If you want to talk about this, I can meet you in an hour."

I didn't know what to say. I must admit that I

21

smiled. But it was because of the man's New York accent. It seemed so strange to hear it coming from an Oriental. Not that it should surprise me. My friend Lucille Yamada at school is Japanese-American, and she talks with a California accent. If there *is* such a thing. But my curiosity was aroused by Suzuki's offer.

"Why are you interested, when Lt. Linderman over there couldn't care less? Isn't it outside your province, too?"

Suzuki smiled, and it made him suddenly handsome — in an exotic way. "Linderman's old guard NYPD," Suzuki said, "and at this time of night, all he's thinking of is getting home. Yes, it's outside my province, but he should have told you who to contact on the chance that you're right about this matter." He looked over at Linderman, who was now gazing at us. "Can't talk now," he said quietly. "Where are you staying?"

"The Plaza."

"Not bad," he said, smiling. "I'll meet you in Trader Vic's, in the lounge in an hour, okay?"

"Errr . . . okay," I said, "but again, why are you interested?"

"I heard you say you were from California. My dad was born there. And for what it's worth, I happen to be left-handed. I know what you meant about the handwriting. Ooops, you better shove off, here comes the lieutenant."

I left quickly before Suzuki got any trouble from his boss.

An hour later, I was sitting in the lounge in Trader Vic's. It's an excellent restaurant in the basement of the Plaza. I couldn't tell you why I was meeting with Detective Suzuki, exactly. Maybe it was because

22

he'd acted friendly toward me, and in New York that counts for a lot. I was fast learning that New York is a chilly town, even in late June. And that has nothing to do with climate.

Despite the late hour, for California, there were couples all around me, talking and laughing, completely involved in themselves. I heard Petunia mention a snack, but I ignored her. I nursed a Seven-Up as the bar had no diet drinks. Just as I was beginning to think Suzuki wouldn't show, I saw him enter the lounge.

At the police station, he'd been in shirtsleeves and wore no tie. Now, he was well turned out in a light-weight sports coat in a muted shade of gray, dark slacks, pale blue shirt and a dark blue tie. He looked more like a graduate student than a policeman. He was scanning the room, looking for me. I waved and caught his eye. He came over to my table and sat down, giving me a bright smile.

"Sorry I'm a bit late, Ms. Fein," he said. "I did have a small *contretemps* with Lt. Linderman, after all."

"About me?" I asked. "I'm sorry, I didn't want you to get in any trouble."

"Not to worry," he said, waving at a waitress. "If it hadn't been this case, it would have been another. Linderman and I don't get along. He's an old timer on the force, and has a low opinion of college-educated cops. Especially one with ambition. He knows that I'm going to law school and resents me."

"For goodness sakes, why?" I asked. "It seems to me that the better educated the policeman, the more effective he'd be."

"Well, good for you!" said Suzuki, grinning widely.

23

"A bit of encouragement like that can see me through a week with Linderman." He took a menu from the waitress and said to me, "Are you hungry? I asked to meet you here because I know they have some genuine Polynesian and Japanese dishes. That, and it's in your hotel."

I heard Petunia grunt approval. "Well, maybe an appetizer . . . " I said.

"Excellent!" said Suzuki. "I know the menu. I waited tables here while I was going to college. Do you mind if I order for us?"

"Not at all," I said. Petunia gave a rousing cheer.

While he ordered, I watched him. Any idea one may have entertained about the classic, impassive, stoic Oriental flew out the window. Suzuki was a true New Yorker, fast moving, fast talking. His face was rarely in repose. His emotions reflected freely in his features. Just now, he was chatting up the waitress about some fellow ex-employees. The waitress evidently knew him well. Once the order was placed and she had gone, he turned to me and said, "Now, as to your problem, Ms. Fein."

I decided to say what was on my mind directly. "Forgive me, Detective Suzuki, but I was wondering what prompted this meeting to begin with. The lieutenant made it clear that this case, if it is one, is outside the province of the New York Police Department."

"It is, and it isn't," he explained. "Strictly speaking, I could have taken Linderman's viewpoint. But law enforcement doesn't stop at a certain point. For instance, if someone is threatening a crowd with a machine gun, a cop doesn't say, 'Automatic weapons

24

possession is a Federal offense. Call the FBI.' The cop does what he must and cooperates with any other agency involved. Don't you see?"

"Well, I think . . . " I began, but he was right back into his ideas of law enforcement.

"And a great many tragedies could be averted if prompt action were taken at all levels. That includes reporting of suspicious circumstances by the civilian population, too. Just as you've done. So, when you went to all the trouble you did at the precinct, I'd have been a poor cop if I didn't give you a fair hearing. Which Linderman didn't."

The hors d'oeuvres arrived. They were hot, and some were served still aflame. There was a Sterno heater in the middle of a large platter, and clustered around it were some of the most glorious-smelling tidbits I'd ever had enchant my nostrils. We spent a few minutes with Suzuki explaining to me what each snack was, and how it was made.

"Of course, these were made up special for us," he said. "I have a little pull around here. Many of the appetizer platters are all prepared, and they just heat them up in the kitchen. Good, but not as good as these."

They were delicious. I tried to restrain Petunia, but in short order, our personalities merged. The plate was bare in minutes. I did have the virtue to decline when Suzuki asked if I wanted any more. He called for a pot of tea, and over the teacups we got back to my problem.

I recounted the events of the day. I tried to remember every detail, even to my spooky, being followed feeling. I threw in my suspicions about my

25

Uncle Claude, too. Suzuki took out a notebook and made notes as I talked. I noticed he used speedwriting. After I'd finished my story, he recapped and began ticking off points one by one. For each of my suspicions, he had a logical explanation. I was beginning to feel a bit less sure that something wrong was happening with my aunt and uncle. If indeed, the man I'd met at the apartment *was* my uncle.

"Now, you're not certain," he was saying, "that the man you met was your Uncle Claude, because he hesitated when you announced yourself?"

"And he had no beard," I added.

"That's nothing," said Suzuki, waving a hand. "Styles change and he could have shaved it off. And who knows what a man looks like underneath a crop of whiskers?"

"And he was evasive about where my aunt was," I said.

"What if he was?" asked Suzuki. "It might have been for a personal reason or a diplomatic reason you knew nothing about. There's a lot of things you wouldn't necessarily know about your aunt and uncle's lives. Like you told me, you haven't seen your aunt since before her marriage, ten years ago. And you've never met your uncle until today . . . "

"If he *was* my uncle," I interjected. "And what about the note that wasn't in her handwriting?"

"I've been thinking about that," Suzuki admitted, "and I've come up with an explanation. Perhaps your uncle wrote it for her. Maybe she wouldn't have had time to get back to their apartment, where the stationery was, and she dictated it to your uncle over the phone."

"Then why didn't he address it to me as from him-self and explain all that?"

"He *is* a diplomat." Suzuki smiled. "Maybe he thought it'd be more personal this way. Nicer and, well, more diplomatic."

"Just a moment, Mr. Suzuki."

"Carl. Call me Carl."

"Then hold on, Carl," I continued. "Are you just giving me a softer version of what I got from your lieutenant? Do you think I'm an irresponsible per-son, seeing burglars under the bed and conspiracies where they aren't?"

"Not at all," he said. "I think you're an extremely intelligent, self-possessed, sensible, and highly attrac-tive young woman. I'm simply playing Devil's Advo-cate here. I'm asking questions that Dakaman secu-rity police will ask you on Monday when you go to the UN. And offering some of the same explanations they will, too."

"Then you do believe me!" I said.

"I believe that you're concerned, and that a lot of what you say makes sense. Actually, most of this can be resolved on Monday. The Dakaman legation will have a recent photo of your uncle. That's what'll resolve the identity question. All the rest of what you've told me is speculative."

Then he gave me that charming smile again. "So we can't do any more tonight. It's nearly twelve-thirty. You've had a big day, you must be exhausted."

"Not at all," I said. "I'm still on Pacific Daylight Time. For me, it's only nine-thirty."

Carl checked his watch. "This city is just getting into full cry about now," he said. "I'm off tomorrow

27

and Monday. Would you like to go somewhere? Or are you put off by going out with a cop? Most New York women are."

"I don't see why," I said quickly. "One of my dear friends in Santa Amelia is the chief of police. We don't share the East Coast attitudes about police in my part of the world. It's just that . . . "

"Or maybe it's the question of race?" Carl offered with a tinge of bitterness I couldn't miss. That's what decided me. All that had been on my mind was to wait in my room until I could call Hawaii long distance. If I called late enough, I'd be sure of getting Mom and Dad in their hotel room.

"The race question never entered my mind," I said easily. "Are you put off by going out with a Caucasian?"

"Touché." Carl Suzuki smiled, waving at the passing waitress. "Where would you like to go?"

"What would you be doing if I weren't with you?" I asked.

"Well, I'm usually at my place on the upper west side, hitting my law books."

"On a Saturday night?" I exclaimed. "No friends, no social life?"

"Are you asking do I have a steady woman friend, Ms. Fein?"

"I certainly am," I said. "No point in mincing about like a kid at the malt shop. I'm of age and my own person, speaking frankly to another person. Are you just being nice, or are you interested in me personally?"

He sat back and blinked. I've heard that policemen tend to be a bit *macho* in man-woman relationships, and I wasn't about to let myself in for an evening of door opening and patronization with him. Even if he was a *verry* attractive man. Just then, the waitress came over with the check. I snared it before Suzuki could, and quickly signed my name and room number. He burst out laughing.

"Sorry, Ms. Fein." He smiled. "Yes, I'm being nice. And it's because I could maybe be interested in you personally. But frankly, I've only known you a few hours. Why don't we call a truce on the war between the sexes and let what happens happen? Deal?" He extended his hand across the table. I shook it.

"Deal!" I said. "Now, where to?"

"How about a disco?" Carl asked. "I know one or two where we might even get in on a Saturday night."

I thought of a disco, and the rock music, which in turn made me think of Larry Small. "I don't think so," I said. "What would you do, if you weren't studying?"

"I don't know if you'd care for it," Carl said, "but I'd probably go to a poolroom I know on Broadway and West 79th Street."

"Now you're talking, cousin!" I cried. "I'd love to go."

"I play very well," he said.

"So do I," I replied. *"Eight Ball,* last pocket, loser pays?"

"Great Scot! I think I'm being hustled!" Carl said, doing an excellent W. C. Fields. It sounded so weird and *outré* coming out of that Japanese face that I broke up.

It was an old-fashioned poolroom. Years and years old, and it smelled funky. But the cues were all

29

straight, and the tables were in superb condition. Carl had his own cue, which he kept at the place. I beat him four games out of nine.

As if by unspoken agreement, we didn't talk about my problem. The conversation was light as meringue, and about as substantial. We talked about books, poetry, art, and shot pool. We laughed a lot. When we left, instead of hailing a taxi, we walked down Broadway. For a while, Carl seemed abstracted. Then he said, "Would you like to walk through the park to the Plaza?"

"I've heard Central Park is quite dangerous at night," I said.

"Are you forgetting you're with a cop?" Carl asked. "This is not a water pistol on my hip, pardner."

"Lead on, sheriff," I said.

As we walked, I noticed how easily we matched pace. Carl is tall for a Japanese, I'd say about five-ten. I'm just five-four. But there was no disparity in our gait. He has an easy, graceful way of moving that makes you feel comfortable. We chatted along the way, and I'm afraid it was mostly about me. He did seem genuinely interested. By the time we'd reached the Plaza, he knew most of what there is to know about me. And I'm ashamed to say, I knew very little about him, save that he was fun, handsome, and easy to be with. On short acquaintanceship, a person really doesn't need much more.

In the lobby, Carl said, "I'll see you to your room, Doris."

Uh-oh, I thought. Here it comes. The obligatory pass. "I'm capable of finding it, Carl," I countered.

"I know you are, Doris," he said, "and I'm not

making advances. If I were, I'd be out in front about it. I want to make sure the room is clear and the corridor empty."

"You mean it's not safe staying at the Plaza?" I squeaked.

"I'm sure it is, ordinarily," he replied, "but you were right about one thing when you told me about today's doings, Doris."

"What's that, for gosh sakes?"

"You're being followed. We both have been since we left here for the poolroom, and all the way back. That's why I took the park walk. I wanted to make sure. He's good, but I spotted him. You have a black man, about six feet tall, a hundred-eighty pounds, wearing a dark blue suit, blue shirt, and maroon tie. He's been with us all night. And if you promise to be cool about not looking right at him, he's standing over there by the revolving door!"

3

Trouble in Dakama

I glanced into one of the many mirrors that line the walls of the Plaza lobby. Sure enough, there he was, exactly as Carl had described him. It may have been my imagination, but I think he noticed me, too. He suddenly became very interested in a showcase for a jewelry store, one of the many exclusive shops located in the hotel.

"See him?" Carl asked.

"Yes, and I think he may have seen me seeing him," I said.

"No matter, now," Carl said. "I told you he's a good shadow. He knew I was on to him when I took us through the park. It may make him cautious. You probably won't see him again."

"How come?"

"Well, if he was a deviate stalking you, being spotted by me would put him off. If there's another reason for his tailing us, it implies an organization. In

32

that case, with one tail exposed, they'll substitute another man we won't recognize."

"An organization?" I said. "What sort of organization?"

"This is New York City," Carl said, steering us toward the elevators, after I'd picked up my key at the desk. "It's the spy capital of the Western Hemisphere. With the UN and every out-of-power faction from countries represented at the UN headquartered here, you can throw a bagel and hit a spy in any crowd. And your uncle *is* political."

The elevator came, and we strolled the corridor after getting off at the eighth floor. When we came to my door, Carl held out his hand. I took it and shook it. He shook his head.

"Lovely handshake, Doris." He grinned. "But I wanted your room key. I want to check the room, too." I handed over the key, and we entered the living room. Everything seemed to be as I left it. Carl went over to the window and looked out over the park.

"First-class view," he said. "Whatever your uncle is, he's not chintzy. This setup goes for more per week than I make in a month. Let me check the bedroom, too."

It stayed at the window, watching hansom cabs enter and exit from the park. After a few seconds, Carl came back and said, "All clear. Now, when I leave, you put the chain on the door and push the double lock button on the knob, like this." He showed me how to lock the door so that even someone with a key couldn't enter. Then he turned and put out his hand.

"I had a great time tonight, Doris," he said.

"So did I, until now," I replied. "But that man in the lobby. It's frightening."

Carl waved his notebook. "I've got all the particulars and his description right here. He knows he's been blown. I don't think you'll have any more problems tonight. If you do . . . " he tore a page out of his notebook, and taking a pen from his pocket wrote quickly. "Here's my home number and address," he said. "I'll be there in about twenty-five minutes. If anything should happen, and I don't think it will, call the desk downstairs immediately, and ask for Security. They'll have a house detective up here faster than a man from the precinct could get here. Then call me. It doesn't matter what time it is, understand? You won't be disturbing me."

"I understand," I said. I wondered what I would do if he wanted to kiss me good night. I've never kissed a Japanese guy. While I was thinking about it, he gave me a cheery wave and was out the door. I didn't know whether I was disappointed or relieved.

It was late now, almost three in the morning. I did some mental arithmetic and figured out that it was still too early in Hawaii for my parents to be in their rooms. Unless, of course, they were changing for dinner. I took the chance and placed the call. Wouldn't you know it? Not there. They'd left word at the desk that the group they were with was taking an air tour of some of the nearby islands. They weren't even on Oahu. I idly flicked on the TV set in the living-room part of the suite. I got the sign-off news from one of the local channels. The newscaster was saying, as a film clip of violent street fighting in some city was being shown: "Repeating the top headlines of the hour, the pitched battle for Dakama City, capital of the newly emerged African republic of Dakama, continues. Rebel forces, which sources say are Cuban armed and equipped, are holding the north end of the city. Fire fights are currently raging for possession of the capitol building which houses the Daruma, the Dakaman legislature. Reports are sketchy, and the UN representative from Dakama could not be reached for comment. More on the Dakama situation as events occur . . . "

The program switched over to local news. I sat there stunned. I didn't hear the rest of the program. It wasn't until the *Star Spangled Banner* played that I crossed over to the set and switched it off. I went into the bedroom. I wanted to reread the letter I'd received in the Oak Room earlier. It wasn't on my bureau where I'd left it! I checked my handbag, but I knew it wasn't there. I remembered clearly that I'd placed it on the bureau when I'd come back from the police station. I even looked behind the bureau. Nothing.

I debated with myself whether I should call Carl Suzuki. Maybe I had misplaced the letter, but no. I knew very well where I'd put it! I got the piece of paper with Carl's number on it and dialed. It rang three times, then I heard Carl's voice say sleepily, "Yeah?"

"Carl, this is Doris Fein . . . "

"Yeah, yeah? What's wrong? Did you call Security?" He was wide awake now.

"It's all right," I said. "No one's breaking down the door. But the letter I got, the one my aunt didn't write, is missing!"

"Are you sure?" he asked.

"Positive," I said. "I left it on the bedroom bureau;

now it's gone. I thought maybe you had taken it when you went into the bedroom."

"Not me, Doris," he said. "Not without asking you." There was silence on the line for a while then.

"Did you watch the late news on TV?" I asked.

"No, I don't have a working TV. Why? What's up?"

I filled him in on the news from Africa. He wanted more details, but I had none to give. "There's a twenty-four-hour news radio station. I can get the scoop from that," he said. "My radio works fine. Let me tune in, then I'll get back to you. Unless you're going to sleep."

"You've got to be kidding!" I replied. "Who could sleep?"

He hung up, and I switched the TV back on. New York stations have all night programming on weekends, I guess. If you could call it that. I was watching a grade-Z technicolor Arabian Nights sword epic with Maria Montez, Jon Hall, and Sabu, when the phone rang. It was Carl.

"Okay," he said without preamble, when I picked up the phone. "Got some of the scoop on Dakama. The radio didn't have much more dope than the TV spot you saw. It seems to be a full-scale revolution going on. It broke out early this morning, our time. If your aunt and uncle are en route to Dakama now, there's no way to check it out. Communications from the capital are spotty, and only a high muckamuck with the government could find out more. I don't think there's anything else we can do tonight, Doris. If you like, I can go with you to the UN tomorrow. It may be Sunday, but things will be popping at the Dakaman legation, I promise you."

"Okay," I said. "What time? How about nine?"

"Give me a break, will you, Doris?" Carl groaned. It's after three now. How about I meet you for breakfast in the Palm Court at . . . say . . . ten-thirty?"

"See you there," I said. "I'll be the spy wearing a hungry expression and carrying a copy of *Time*."

"Glad you said that." Carl laughed. "I might not have recognized you. When I was a kid, I had trouble telling white folks apart. You all look alike, you know."

Despite the events of the day, I had no trouble sleeping. It all hit me in a few minutes after I'd taken a hot bath. But before I did, I made sure the door locks were in place. Even on the bathroom door. But I always lock the bathroom door in hotels. I never got over seeing *Psycho* on TV.

* * *

Carl had the Sunday *New York Times* with him when he showed up, exactly on time. I was feeling quite tired. I suppose that all the events of yesterday had generated enough excitement that I hadn't noticed being fatigued. I was glad he had brought the paper. I don't think I could have carried it! I've seen the L.A. *Times* look more than substantial on weekends, but the *New York Times* on a Sunday is not to be believed. Carl sat down and helped himself to coffee from the pot I was working on.

"Here's what the *Times* has to say about the Dakama revolution. Incidentally, that's what they're calling it: a revolution. Not an uprising or insurrection," he said.

"Well, good morning to you, too!" I said.

"I'm sorry," Carl said, "my thoughts were so much on the problem at hand. I was less than social, I'm afraid. Care to start again? Good morning, Doris, you look marvelous. How do you feel?"

"As though I was worked over by Ken Norton," I replied. "It all caught up with me this morning. I could barely get out of bed."

"Jet lag." Carl smiled. "It may be ten-thirty here, but your internal clock is still on West Coast time. It's seven-thirty to you, physically."

"That's not early," I protested. "I get up at this time, or I should say this time *back there,* every day."

"Sure," Carl agreed, "but not after going to bed at the equivalent of two hours before. No wonder you're beat. Have you ordered yet?"

"I was waiting for you," I explained. "I thought you might be able to get us a special breakfast, seeing as how you have all the friends at this hotel."

"Not in this place," Carl said. "Just downstairs in Trader Vic's. It's an entirely different operation. Down there, they like to have Orientals waiting tables. The Palm Court is . . . different, let's say."

"The racial question, as you call it?" I asked.

"Not a question at all. A fact of life," said Carl. "But not a bad problem. Not on this coast, anyway."

"Meaning it is in California?"

"I'd suppose so, from all I've heard from my father and other relatives," he said. "Of course, my father had a jaundiced view of California, no pun intended. He spent a part of World War Two in a concentration camp in Arizona."

"Oh," I said, "he was in an internment camp."

This was something I knew about. In 1942, just

after World War Two began, our government rounded up all the Japanese-Americans on the West Coast and shipped them to internment camps, far inland. The feeling was, back then, that if the Japanese Imperial Army ever landed on the West Coast, all the loyal Japanese-Americans would rise up and help them! Can you imagine such nonsense? To make it worse, no German-Americans or Italian-Americans were interned.

"Internment camp?" snorted Carl. "That's a nice way of putting it. Say it like it was, Doris. It was prison camp, concentration camp . . . jail. My poor dad was taken away. He was born in Los Angeles, and the most political he ever got was to vote for Franklin D. Roosevelt in 1940!"

"And he spent the war in a . . . concentration camp?"

"No, he volunteered for the army. Fought in Europe and won a bunch of medals." Carl smiled ruefully. "Then, when he was wounded and sent home, he got permission to visit his folks, who were still in that jail in Arizona. Can you imagine? He needed *permission*. A war hero!"

"It does sound outrageous," I said, "but that was back then . . . "

"So it's all right to forget it?" Carl said heatedly. "I still recall my dad telling me what it was like. He went out to Arizona and his kid sister, my aunt Kimiko, said to him, 'Brother, can we go home now? I don't like it here in Japan.' "

"I don't understand," I said.

"My aunt was only seven years old," Carl explained. "Before 1943, she'd never seen many Japa-

39

nese people. My folks lived in a mostly Caucasian town. When they went to Arizona, she thought they'd all been sent to Japan!"

I sat silently. What can you say to something like that?

"But we're here to talk about your aunt, not mine," Carl said.

That brought me back to the present quickly enough. I'd been so involved with what Carl had been telling me that I'd momentarily forgotten. We ordered breakfast, and while we waited Carl filled me in on what was happening in Dakama. According to the Sunday *Times*.

"Apparently there are two factions in Dakama," he began. "One party is in power now, with the blessing of the U.S. government. And that party is biracial. But after a number of years of small outbreaks of violence, the Dakaman government is gradually shifting to black rule. The blacks outnumber the whites in Dakama by about twenty to one."

"I know," I volunteered. "Uncle Claude was instrumental in the changeover."

"Well, the changeover isn't going fast enough for the party that's *out* of power," Carl explained. "And the out-of-powers feel that any blacks holding office in Dakama now are white man's toadies. They want an all-black government and death to the white . . . imperialist devils!"

"Sounds familiar," I said. "They said that in Vietnam."

"I know," said Carl, "and from the same sources. But the Viet Cong were bankrolled by the Russians. This outfit in Dakama may be backed by the Cubans, according to The *Times*. And from all reports, they're making the Viet Cong look like pussycats. Look at this."

He handed me a feature story about the fighting in Dakama. It seemed that the insurgents were taking no prisoners. The atrocity tales were reminiscent of too many of the reports from Southeast Asia. "Brrr!" I said.

"Brrr, indeed," added Carl. "If your aunt and uncle are in Dakama City right now, I don't envy them. My radio said there might even be more Cuban troops going to Dakama soon. Our State Department is up in the air about that, you can bet."

The breakfast arrived, and we switched over to less depressing topics of conversation. I learned that Carl's father was retired and living in Florida, near St. Petersburg. And that he has two brothers, both older than he. One married and living on Long Island. He's an accountant. The other brother is a full colonel in the U.S. Army, in Germany. His mother died five years ago.

Carl was only ten credits away from his law degree, and was going to NYU Law, in Greenwich Village.

He'd been very astute in his studies and his career goals as well. He was planning on going with the district attorney's staff once he passed his bar examination.

"And then what?" I asked him.

"And then, I'll play it by ear," he said. "Watch for an opportunity and seize the moment to my purpose."

"Which is?"

"Promise not to laugh?"

"Solemn vow," I said, holding up my right hand.

"I think I'd like to be in Congress," he said. "It's time, I think. There are Senators Inouye and Matsunaga from Hawaii. Inouye fought in Europe with my dad, you know."

"I didn't know."

"They didn't know each other well," Carl said. "But when Inouye was on TV during the Watergate investigations, Dad wrote him a letter. Got a nice answer too. Dad told him about me and my political ambitions. He wrote back to Dad that when I was ready to make my move, he'd like to meet me."

"Why, that's wonderful, Carl!"

"Yeah, maybe," he said, finishing his coffee. "But politicians are politicians. Think about it. Some guy from your old outfit in WW Two writes to you about his son with political aspirations, what can you write back? Get lost? Nah, that letter isn't anything I'd try to borrow money on. But it was nice of him. If we Japanese-Americans are nothing else, we're polite."

"I still think it's a great letter," I persisted.

"Speaking of letters," Carl said, "did you ever find the one from your aunt?"

"Allegedly from my aunt, Mr. District Attorney," I sniped. "And no, I didn't. It's not misplaced, either. That letter was taken from my room!"

"Could have been our friend from last night," Carl mused. "While you were down in Vic's, with me. He'd have had time to break into your room, get the letter and still be back at Vic's in time to tail us."

"But who is he? Why is he doing this?" I asked.

Carl shrugged. "Please, lady, I'm just a New York cop, not that famous Japanese detective, *Mr. Moto*. I don't think we'll know the game, let alone the score, until we talk to somebody at the Dakama group at the UN. You ready to go?"

I finished my last sip of coffee. Black, with Sweet 'n Low. I was still guilty over my Petunia lapse last night. This time, Carl grabbed the check. I didn't mind. So far, we were even up on paying. I was ready to stop at the cab stand outside the Plaza, but Carl steered me into the street, and we soon were walking briskly toward the East Side. When I asked why, he replied, "Cabs cost a fortune, and I'm just a humble civil servant, Doris. I can't afford breakfasts at the Palm Court and a cab to the UN too. We'll take the subway."

We got the subway three blocks away. Right across the street from Bloomingdale's. Being Sunday, the store was closed.

I'd never been on a subway train, and, in retrospect, I could do without ever being on one again. The subway was all it's been made out to be: noisy, dirty, and about the fastest, cheapest way to go anywhere in Manhattan. Conversation *was* possible over the roar of the train, but only by leaning close to each other and virtually speaking directly into each other's ear. I was just leaning over to say something to Carl, when he abruptly stood up.

"Whooops! Here's 42nd Street. Our stop!" he added. We'd been talking and self-involved. The subway car doors were closing. I would have stepped back and ridden to the next station. But Carl is a New Yorker. He grabbed the closing door and held it as I squeaked by and onto the platform. Then he joined me. He was laughing.

"Lost him!" he crowed. "He probably never saw *The French Connection*. I shook him perfectly!"

"What *are* you talking about?"

"Our new tail," Carl said, still grinning widely. "Five-ten, very young exec, tan three-piece business suit, striped tie. Hispanic, I'd say. That's why we took the subway, Doris. A cab following another cab in Manhattan is hard to spot. It's the law that they're all painted yellow. But on foot, or in the subway, it's easier to spot someone tailing you. So when our stop came up, I didn't make a move for the door until it was closing. Caught our friend flat-footed, you should excuse the expression."

"This isn't happening," I said, mostly to myself. "I'm on a vacation, not getting involved in plots. This isn't my style."

"A bit late to be uninvolved," Carl said. "Our tail on the train is no dummy. When we got off at 42nd Street, I'm sure he figured where we're headed. By the time we walk over to the UN, he'll probably be waiting for us!"

4

At the UN

The Dakaman Legation office was a madhouse. We'd been waiting in the outside reception area for two hours while a steady stream of people of all colors and descriptions flowed in and out. It seemed everyone had priority over Carl and me to see Selim Bakka, the chief Dakaman representative to the UN. I'd explained who I was to the receptionist, a strikingly beautiful black woman with a French accent that added to her attractiveness.

"I am so sorry," she'd said, "but relatives and immediate families of Dakaman nationals in Dakama will be notified of any casualties from the fighting once we receive casualty lists. And so far, we know little."

"Then we'd like to see Ambassador Bakka," I said.

"For what purpose?" asked the receptionist. "You must understand that the ambassador is swamped with callers. And he, himself, may be flying to Dakama this evening."

I debated telling this woman about my suspicions. For one thing, she'd probably think me a crackpot. I couldn't use Carl's status as a police officer. He wasn't with me in an official capacity. And as Lt. Linderman had told me many times the evening before, this matter was outside the NYPD's jurisdiction in any event.

"I want to make sure that my aunt and uncle are, in fact, in Dakama City," I replied.

The receptionist sighed deeply and took a piece of memo paper from a holder on her desk. "What was the name again?" she asked.

"Fein, Doris Fein. I'm the niece of Claude Bernard," I said. "You do know who he is, don't you?" I added maliciously. Maybe the woman hadn't heard me earlier. Her face lit up in recognition. Then I realized that when we'd spoken earlier, I'd pronounced my uncle's name in the anglicized manner, BURR-nard. After hearing her French accent, this time I'd said Bear-NAHR.

"*Attendez, Mademoiselle* Fein," she said. "You refer to our Economic Secretary?"

"If that's what he is," I said. "He's my uncle by marriage. We've nev . . . " I almost said that we'd never met, as I was convinced by now that the man I'd talked with at the apartment was not my uncle. "We'd never met before yesterday," I finished. "When I last saw him, he said that he and my aunt were headed for Dakama City." I saw her take a breath. She was about to go into the same spiel she gave us earlier about no reports. I cut her off. "I'm not trying to get a report on them from Dakama. I just want to know if they actually did leave last night."

"One moment," the receptionist said, and pressed a key on the intercom. I heard a bass voice say, *"Oui?"* Then she and the voice went into a rapid-fire dialogue in French. It was too fast for me to follow. After a few seconds, the receptionist favored us with a brilliant smile. "The ambassador will see you. This way, please."

The reception area door opened onto an inner office that housed a number of doorless cubicles. Sunday or not, each occupant was engaged in frenetic activity, telephoning, dictating into machines, or scanning papers. A woman who could have been the twin of the receptionist was seated at a desk outside a big oaken door. The door had the legend *Ambassador S. Bakka* written on it in French, English, and, I assume, it said the same thing in Arabic. The twin of our guide got up and opened the big door and showed us in without a word.

The office was done in African Modern, if there is such a style; deep pile lime-green carpets, furniture in rattan with African print fabric. There were masks and spears on the walls, and framed in the same rattan were a portrait of a very fat black man in full tribal regalia of some sort, and a huge map of the Republic of Dakama.

Seated behind an elaborate desk that had the most fantastic inlays I've ever seen, was a very dark-skinned black man. He stood as we entered, and I could see he was of average height. He was wearing the diplomat's uniform: a Savile Row business suit, pale shirt and a tie I *think* I recognized as an English public school pattern.

"Ah, *Mademoiselle* Fein," he said in an Oxonian accent, laid over French, "we meet under unfortunate circumstances, I'm afraid. I am Selim Bakka, Ambassador Plenipotentiary to the UN. I understand that you are Claude Bernard's niece?"

I took his proffered hand and gave it a European shake: one firm downward movement. "A pleasure to meet you, Mr. Ambassador," I said. "Yes, I'm *Monsieur* Bernard's niece. Actually, his wife, Lois, is my mother's sister. This is my friend, Detective Carl Suzuki, of the New York City Police."

The ambassador raised his eyebrows when I mentioned police. But in a split second, he was all charm. *"Ohiro gozaimas, Suzuki-san,"* he purred in the same rich basso I'd heard over the intercom.

"Good morning, sir," Carl answered. "You'll have to excuse my lack of refinement, but I speak very little Japanese."

"Ah, then you are *Nisei?*" asked the ambassador.

"No, your Excellency, *Sansei,*" Carl replied.

"Ah so, des'ka." Bakka smiled. "Then English is the order of the day, eh?"

"Only if we're going to understand each other." Carl smiled.

"Then tell me," Bakka said smoothly, "how I may help you?"

I quickly recapped the events of yesterday. Leaving nothing out, including Carl's spotting the two men who had shadowed us. Bakka listened in silence, nodding once in a while to indicate he understood. I finished by saying, "So you see, your Excellency, I don't know for sure that Aunt Lois and Uncle Claude are in Dakama City. I don't even know for sure if the man I met at the East 79th Street apartment *was* my Uncle Claude!"

"Well that, at least, is easily resolved," said Bakka. He pushed a button on his desktop intercom and spoke in a language I couldn't recognize. A female voice — I assume it was the woman at the desk outside — replied in the same language. Bakka noted my look and said to me, "I can see, Ms. Fein . . . Do you prefer the feminist honorific?"

"*Mademoiselle* or Ms.," I said, "it's all the same to me."

"Well, *Mademoiselle* Fein, I can see you are puzzled by my use of language. Allow me to clarify. There are many languages spoken in my country. Though we are among the newest of the emergent nations, the kingdom of Dakama is ancient. Some believe that Dakama is the legendary kingdom of Prester John. The country is divided into three parts, as you can see . . . " Bakka got up and walked over to the big map on the wall and pointed gracefully. "Here is the seacoast on the Atlantic. The seaports are our major cities. You will find that French is the primary language here, along with Arabic. Before Dakama fell under French rule after World War One, we were subjects of the Sultan of Turkey. In fact, our official religion is Islam." He indicated a section of the map farther inland. "Now here, in the mountains, and where Dakama City is located, the languages spoken are Arabic, some French, and my own native tongue, Dakaman." He pointed again. "In the interior, where our new-found mineral wealth is located — some historians say it's the location of King Solomon's mines — is where the bulk of our true black African population lives. The hill people and seacoast peoples are admixtures of black, Semitic, and Caucasian. Dakama City is located centrally so that it serves as the capital for all the back-country tribesmen as well as the more western population. I am from the back country, and . . . "

There was a knock at the door. *"Entrez,"* Bakka said, and the beautiful black woman came in with a bulky file under her arm. Bakka took the file, thanked her in the other language and turned to us. He consulted the file for a second and removed a photograph. "Now, *Mademoiselle* Fein," he smiled, "is this a photograph of the man you met yesterday?"

I looked at the picture. It could have been the man. I say *could* have, because the man in the photo wore a full beard. "I can't say for sure," I told Bakka. "The man I met had no beard. But surely, you've seen my uncle recently. More recently than this picture, haven't you?"

Bakka looked uneasy. The first time in our interview he didn't seem completely at ease. "To be sure," he said. "I see Bernard once a month, at our regular full staff meetings. But in his capacity as Economic Secretary. We rarely meet socially. I last saw him in late May. He had a beard then."

"But he could have shaved it since then, Mr. Ambassador?" asked Carl. "And you wouldn't have known about it?"

"Mr. Suzuki. I have many, many duties as ambassador. And to a certain extent, mission gossip is my stock in trade. But the shaving habits of the Economic Secretary . . . " he spread his hands and lifted his shoulders. "But wait." He smiled. "We can find out quite easily. I'll call his secretary."

Bakka crossed over to his desk, and I noticed that he carefully placed the file he held in such a way as neither Carl nor I could glance at it without craning our necks. He spoke into the intercom, again in Dakaman. In a second, the telephone on his desk rang. He spoke French this time. He hung up the phone and said to us, "This is assuming comic proportions, I think. Claude Bernard's secretary is not in the building. When the hostilities broke out, we canceled all holidays for mission personnel and called them to the office. But Bernard's secretary couldn't be reached. No one knows where he is."

"But there must be someone else who has seen Bernard in the past few days?" Carl asked.

Selim Bakka smiled. "Many. But you must admit this means nothing. There is no grooming code among our people. Bernard wouldn't serve notice upon us, nor seek our permission to shave his beard. He could have just finished shaving when you saw him yesterday, *Mademoiselle* Fein."

"Back to square one," I said glumly.

"Not at all." Bakka smiled again. "I also inquired about his departure for Dakama. Understandably, our national airline wasn't functioning to Dakama City. Transportation division reserved two Pan-American tickets to El Jaziz, on the Dakaman seacoast. I understand that the tickets were picked up personally by Claude Bernard yesterday at seven

51

P.M. I think we may safely say that your aunt and uncle are somewhere in Dakama at this very moment. I trust this allays your fears, Mademoiselle Fein?"

I was going to say more, but Carl interrupted. "It certainly does, your Excellency. Sorry to have taken up so much of your time."

"Not at all, Suzuki-*san*," Bakka said. "Bernard is one of Dakama's most valued citizens. His family is of great import to us. And *Mademoiselle* Fein?"

"Yes, your Excellency?"

"As soon as we here at the mission receive any word about your aunt and uncle, we will notify you. You'll be staying on at your hotel?"

"Yes, the Plaza, for another two weeks," I replied.

"Then I would do as your uncle advised," said Bakka smoothly. "Enjoy the city and your vacation. Perhaps the current difficulties will soon be resolved, and your aunt and uncle will be back."

Before we realized it, Bakka had steered us to the door, and we were being led back out to the reception area by his secretary.

Outside the building, Carl and I walked through the rose gardens that face the East River. The gardens were beautiful, but I was in no frame of mind to enjoy them. I had gone along with Carl when he'd cut me off in Bakka's office. I was quickly finding out that Carl seemed to have reasons, and good ones, each time he did something I didn't understand. I asked him why he had ducked out of the interview.

"Because I saw we weren't going to get any real information, Doris," he said. "We got a swell geography and history lesson on Dakama. We were told a lot of stuff we already knew, and not one iota of

52

information that would confirm or deny your suspicions. If there's something going on, that man, Bakka, is in on it!"

"I don't follow all this," I said, my head spinning. "He's part of Uncle Claude's government. Uncle Claude's boss, in fact."

"He's also a black Dakaman," Carl noted. "And that's the root of the revolution that's going on in Dakama right now, remember?"

"Oh, no!" I said. "Do you think there's a *coup d'état* in process, and that Bakka is part of it?"

"I don't know, I just don't know," Carl said. "But he did drop a piece of information we could check on. He said that your relatives left on a Pan-Am flight for El Jaziz, in Dakama, at some hour later than seven last night. There can't be that many flights to Dakama. We can check with the airline and see if they were on the plane!"

"How can you check that out?" I asked.

"Simple," Carl said. "I'll wave my badge at someone at the Fifth Avenue office of Pan-Am. They'll check the office at the airport, and we'll know right away. Come on, let's grab a cab."

"I'll pay," I said. "You don't have all that much money."

"It's not that far,"Carl smiled. "But if you insist on paying . . ."

* * *

I sat watching Carl throw his official weight at a platinum blonde, polyethylene beauty at the Pan-Am desk. I idly leafed through some magazines. He came back to where I was sitting in a few moments. and his expression was grim.

"Well, *somebody* took the flight," he said to me as we left, "but what the people looked like, the airport help couldn't say. The clerk who was at the boarding area last night isn't at Kennedy today. It's his day off."

"Rats!" I said. "When will he be back on duty?"

"Not until Tuesday, Doris," Carl said. "But don't despair. I got the clerk's home phone and address. He lives in Manhattan, down in the Village, not far from where I go to school. I'll call and see if I can get him at home. Let's find a pay phone. I could have called from the desk at the Pan-Am office, but it wasn't private."

We found a street phone, and I window-shopped at the Gucci salon on Fifth Avenue while Carl made his call. I was eyeing a particularly chic set of matched luggage when he tapped me on the shoulder. I nearly jumped out of my skin. All this intrigue was getting to me.

"He's home," Carl said triumphantly. "We're to meet him at a place called The Cauldron on Mac-Dougal Street in Greenwich Village in an hour and a half!"

"Couldn't he tell you anything over the phone?" I asked.

"You don't know New Yorkers," Carl laughed. "They're not easily conned. My saying on the phone that I'm a cop doesn't mean a thing. He won't open up unless he sees the badge."

"Badges?" I said, in my best *Treasure of Sierra Madre* Mexican-bandit accent. Carl knew the picture, because he chorused the rest of the line with me. "We don't need no dirty stinkin' badges!"

We spent the subway ride to Greenwich Village throwing lines from Humphrey Bogart movies at each other. We were doing lines from *Casablanca* when Carl suddenly fell silent.

"What's wrong, Carl?" I asked.

"We've got company again, Doris," he said grimly. "Only this time, there's two of them!"

5

Kidnapped!

The Cauldron turned out to be a seamy combination of Italian restaurant and neighborhood bar. It was on a street that positively exuded local cops. MacDougal Street is one of the main drags in Greenwich Village, and on a warm Sunday afternoon in June, the freak count among the pedestrians is high. There were artsy types of all sexes, some indeterminate. I was so wrapped up in gawking that I accidently discovered why New Yorkers seldom look you in the eye on the street. It seems most of them walk with their eyes focused on the ground in front of them. Doggie-doo. I was watching a particularly hairy young man with a guitar slung over his shoulder when I stepped in something: one guess what.

I was mortally embarrassed, but Carl laughed it off. "Congratulations!" he chortled. "You are now officially a New Yorker." I was so glad I hadn't worn my sandals. Carl showed me how to scrape the residue off against a curbstone. As I did so, he said, "That move is called the Manhattan Sidestep. Since the new cleanup law, it's a disappearing motion. But there are still people who don't clean up after their pets."

"I've noticed," I remarked drily, as we entered the front door of The Cauldron.

We were early for our appointment with the airline clerk, so we took a table, not far from the kitchen. In fact, all the tables were close to the open kitchen. There was a longish bar, then the kitchen, and clustered around the cooking area was a series of tables and chairs. The bartender came from behind the bar and took our orders. Seven-Up for me, a beer for Carl.

The place was old. The walls were covered with paintings of doubtful merit and yellowed photographs in frames. The pictures were of eminently forgettable noncelebrities, all of whom seemed to own guitars. I did recognize a few faces, though. Peter, Paul and Mary and Bob Dylan. I was excited about that, but Carl explained.

"Years ago, during the folk music boom, this place was quite popular. That was only because it's the closest bar to the places where the performing cafés used to be. Most of them are gone now. And I don't think there's been a celebrity in this joint since 1968. They sort of coast on past glories."

"The food smells good, though," I said. I heard Petunia grunt assent, and remembered I hadn't eaten lunch.

"Oh, it is," said Carl. "I have dinner here twice a week when school is in session. But I don't think they serve lunch."

"It's not important," I lied gallantly. "I'm not hungry."

"Tell you what," Carl said, "after we talk with this guy," he checked his notebook, "Maloney, William Maloney, I'll take you somewhere for lunch. Okay?"

"Great," I said. "By the way, how will you know Maloney when you see him?"

"Shouldn't be hard," Carl said. "He described himself over the phone. And he'll know us. I told him there were two of us and said he should look for a very lovely brunette with green eyes and a worried-looking Japanese man about thirty."

"Why thank you, Carl," I said. "Wouldn't it have been easier to say I was short and overweight? Gallantry is fine, but a good description goes a longer way."

"Overweight?" Carl said, and I could have kissed him, "I don't think so. Maybe I have the famous Japanese predilection for full-bodied women, but I'd hardly call you overweight."

"Tell me more about the predilection," I said, leaning across the table, "and when the next flight leaves for Japan!"

"You don't get away that easy," he laughed. "But it's true, you know. Many Japanese men go crazy for women of your, er . . . build."

"Fascinating country, Japan," I said dreamily. "I must visit it soon."

"Don't grab a plane just yet," Carl said. "I think our Mr. Maloney just came in."

William Maloney was the most handsome man I've ever seen outside of TV or the movies. He was impeccably dressed in a cashmere sport coat, turtleneck sweater, tweed slacks, Gucci loafers, and an Irish tweed crush hat. The colors ranged from chocolate brown to fawn. He had clear blue eyes and jet black hair that peeked out below his hat, barely brushing the color of his tan turtleneck sweater. I don't think he ever had a pimple in his life. I sat there, open-mouthed as this gorgeous man walked over to our table. He'd evidently recognized us from Carl's description.

"Mr. Suzuki? Ms. Fein?" he asked. My heart nearly broke. Maloney was beautiful all right. But if his speech pattern, complete to sibilant *esses* was any indication, Mr. Maloney was also stone gay. That's the way it goes, I thought. All the beautiful ones are either taken or gay. Not that Carl Suzuki isn't handsome; he is, very. I suppose I looked at Maloney in the same way Petunia would eye a hot-fudge sundae at Baskin-Robbins: sweet, beauteous, and completely out of the question.

Carl got right down to cases with Maloney. He showed his badge and asked, "Now, Mr. Maloney, you were on duty last night at Pan-Am Gate 132?"

"I was," Maloney replied. "And I checked in all the passengers for the nine-thirty P.M. flight to El Jaziz and Casablanca. Dakama is a stopover. The flight terminates in Casablanca."

"You must remember this," I hummed. Carl gave me a no-no look.

"Do you remember seeing two Caucasians, both in their forties, ticketed for Dakama? Their names would be Claude and Lois Bernard. Traveling on diplomatic passports."

"The passports aren't my responsibility; I wouldn't have seen them," Maloney said. "But I do recall a couple of that general description. And yes, the name would be Bernard, I think."

"Good, good," Carl said. "Now this is important. Do you recall what the man looked like?"

"I surely do," said Maloney. "He was quite handsome, and had a charming French accent. Very well dressed, and, of course, I'd remember his attaché case."

"Really? Why?" Carl asked.

"That's how I know he was a diplomat of some sort. His attaché case was handcuffed to his wrist," said Maloney. "And, of course, he had a beard. Easily remembered."

"He *did* have a beard?" I broke in. "What did the woman look like?"

"Brunette, about forty, slightly chubby . . . "

"That's Aunt Lois!" I said excitedly. "They did get on the plane!"

"I *told* you that," said Maloney impatiently. "Will there be anything else? And what's this all about, may I ask?"

"Missing persons report, purely routine," Carl said.

"Well, if they were who you're interested in, they're hardly missing. They've been in Dakama since this morning at . . . " he checked his watch, "eight A.M. New York time. Will that be all, Mr. Suzuki? I have an engagement."

"Yes, thank you. You've been very helpful," Carl said.

"Anything I can do to help our boys in blue," said Maloney, smiling. "I've found *some* of New York's finest to be just that!"

Maloney ignored my hand as he got up, but shook Carl's. I would have made a remark, but what for? In a moment, he was gone. Soon as he left, I said to Carl, "Bingo! The man who got on the plane wasn't the man I met!"

"Not unless he grew a full beard in three hours," Carl said. "And that neatly places your aunt and uncle in Dakama. There is only one mystery remaining. Who was the stranger at their apartment, and why did Selim Bakka lie to us?"

"Lie? When did he do that?" I asked.

"All through our interview," Carl responded. "He was throwing dust in our eyes every step of the way. Oh, he's smooth. But after all, he's a diplomat. Intrigue is his line of work. Man, the way he dropped that little tidbit about Pan-Am. I rose like a trout to a fly! He knew I'd check it out."

"But how do you know he was lying for sure?" I asked, taken aback.

"Doris, you have to pay close attention to *how* people say things, as well as what they say," Carl said. "And close attention to the things they leave out and include. Then you stack it up against those things you know to be true. For instance, do you remember what Bakka said when we left his office?"

I thought back. "Sure. He told me to enjoy the city, and that my aunt and uncle might be back soon."

"Right," Carl said, "but you overlooked one thing. I didn't. He said to enjoy the city, *as your uncle had advised you*. That wasn't what you had told Bakka. The advice to enjoy the city was in the note, supposedly from your aunt. And you never mentioned being told that in the letter. You simply said that the letter advised you that your relatives couldn't make it for dinner and would be flying out earlier than planned. It was *Bakka* who quoted your 'uncle,' not you!"

"You're right!" I squeaked. "But what do we do now?"

"Well," Carl said, "we could go back to the apartment on 79th Street, ring the bell and see who answers."

"Let's go then!"

"Whoa, whoa," Carl said. "You don't go without a plan, and although you may get by on nervous energy, *this* army travels on its stomach. The apartment won't go away, and it's way past lunchtime. What about some Japanese food? I know a decent place up on 8th Street."

"I'm too excited to eat," I protested, but I was wrong. Petunia helped me.

The restaurant was called The Sakura, which, Carl explained, means Cherry Blossom. It was small, with ordinary tables and chairs. When we went in, Carl walked right by the tables and toward the back of the room. I wondered what was going on, until I saw there was another dining room. An elderly, graceful Japanese woman dressed in a kimono greeted Carl warmly. And in Japanese! Carl immediately ran off a string of Japanese in reply that had my head twirling. Especially after he'd said he didn't speak Japanese. He finished gossiping with the Japanese woman, and, even though I don't understand a word of the language, it was obvious that he was introducing the two of us. I caught the *Doris Fein* part, anyhow. Then Carl said to me, "Doris, this is Mrs. Yamashina. She's a distant cousin of mine."

"Howareya, dearie?" said Mrs. Yamashina in rich Brooklynese. "This little stinker never comes to see me any more. At least, this time he brought somebody nice with him, insteada a buncha cops."

"Delighted to meet you, Mrs. Yamashina," I said, and tried a small bow.

"Good manners, too," said Mrs. Yamashina to Carl. Then to me, "Lucille's the name, chickie. Call me Lucille. Ya hungry?"

"That's why we came, Lucille," Carl said. "And to see you, of course."

"Then see what Harry has left from lunch hour in the kitchen," Lucille said. "You know this place as well as I do. And when you pass the bar, you can bring me a bourbon and water."

Mrs. Yamashina turned to me and asked, "How about a little drink, Dorothy?"

"Doris," I corrected. "Maybe I'll take a little Diet Pepsi . . . "

Lucille shrugged visibly. "How can you drink that moose pee? At least have a glass of Chablis. I hate drinking alone." I agreed to a Chablis, and Carl left for the kitchen.

Lucille led me into the private room. It was a *tatami* room, a traditional Japanese dining area, with grass mats on the floor and a very low table. Lucille sat down easily as water flows down a hillside. I puffed and groaned my way into an ungraceful version of Lucille's sitting position.

"Carl!" Lucille roared, "where's the drinks? Get

your buns in here. I want to hear about your family!" Mrs. Yamashina turned to me and said, "When he was little, I couldn't keep him out of this joint. Now, he's a big-time cop, I hardly see him at all."

"What are you talking about, Lucille?" asked Carl, entering with two glasses. "I had dinner here last week."

"Yeah, and who'd you bring for guests? Cops!" Lucille snorted.

Carl shed his shoes, and sat down gracefully at the low table. It made me ashamed of all the grunting and groaning it had taken me to get into the same position. Somehow, in these surroundings, Carl looked much more Japanese.

"Lucille doesn't like cops," Carl said, somewhat superfluously. "She's a horse player. And even with Off-Track Betting in New York, she still supports a half dozen bookies."

"Only three." Lucille laughed. "Don't exaggerate. And I use them for ball games and fights. OTB doesn't cover those things. Does that make me a criminal?"

"Technically, yes," Carl said. "And if this lunch isn't any good, I'm liable to bust you, Lucille!"

She roared with laughter. "That'll be the day, you little stinker! How do you bust somebody who used to change your diapers, huh? Tell me that!"

Carl caught my look when Lucille mentioned diapers. "Lucille used to be my baby-sitter years ago, when Dad had his restaurant on 50th Street. She was a showgirl at the *Copacabana* back then."

"Showgirl?" squeaked Lucille. "I was featured *dance-youse,* and don't you forget it! I usedta eat

64

lunch at Carl's father's greasy spoon, Doris. First time I seen his wife trying to take care of customers and still watch the stinker here, my heart almost broke. So I figure, what the hey, I got my days free. I can watch the kid. And in those days, we was all being Chinese . . . it kept us tight together, I guess."

"I told you about the Chinese dodge," Carl said.

"Yes, you did," I said. "And I think it's scandalous having to pretend such a thing. It's denying what you really are!"

"Good for you, honey," said Lucille, patting my hand. "But you gotta understand. A lotta people lost friends and family in the war. And being Japanese wasn't too popular. It was easier if someone asked to say you was Chinese." For a second, she seemed far away. Then she turned to me and said, "Now that I think of it, what about you, honey? Is your real name Fein? Or was it Feinstein or Feinberg once upon a time?"

I turned deep red. I happen to know that when my father's grandfather came to the United States from Germany in 1902, we *were* Feinsteins. The family changed the name during World War One, so folks wouldn't think they were Germans. "Feinstein," I murmured.

"So there you are, honey," crowed Lucille. "Now, whaddaya want to eat?"

Perhaps it was because Carl was "family" or just because I was so hungry, but the meal was exquisite. It bore the same relationship to Benihana that Maxim's in Paris does to McDonald's. I'm a big fish eater, and by the time we'd done with the meal, both Petunia and I were breathing through gills.

We finished the meal, and Carl walked and I waddled to the door.

"Now don't be a stranger, now you know where we are, honey," Lucille said to me. "You're the first decent company I've seen the stinker with. You sure you gotta go back to California?"

"Positive," I said. "School starts up in the fall."

"Ah, college!" she said deprecatingly. "I never went to college. And I did all right."

"You probably had a better figure, Lucille," I countered.

"What kind of better?" she said, pinching my behind. "A showgirl is one thing. But a man gets married, he don't want a skinny broad he's gotta shake the sheets to find! You'll do all right, sweetie."

I saw that it was no time to explain to Lucille that I feel a woman should have options in her life that are more rewarding than dancing half-clothed or keeping house. But Lucille and I were separated by more than cultures.

We said some long, drawn-out good-byes, then headed for the subway. I was anxious to ask Carl a few questions, too. We hadn't been able to talk about much with Lucille in constant attendance. Once we were on the subway, Carl asked, "Well, what do you think of Lucille?"

"She's marvelous!" I said. "I've met some unusual people, too."

"Funny, I don't consider Lucille unusual," Carl said. "She's always been a fact of life for me."

"Oh, I didn't mean it in a deprecatory way, Carl," I said hurriedly. "I meant that she's one of life's bigger-than-life characters. I know a very old man in

Santa Amelia, for instance. He's fabulously wealthy. He owns a newspaper, but he works on it as a reporter. His name is Harry Grubb. You should meet him, someday."

"If he's in your hometown that doesn't seem likely," Carl said.

"He comes to New York twice a year," I told Carl. "He buys all his clothes and furnishings here. Says he can't find a good conservative business suit in California. Too jazzy for him, as he puts it. I'll give him your number to call next time. If that's all right with you."

"I don't know how much I'd have in common with a Caucasian millionaire," Carl said.

"As much as I do with a Japanese chorus girl, I'd guess. But I got on fine with Lucille. And Harry Grubb talks your language. He was a police reporter."

"Okay, okay." Carl laughed. "Give him my number. But you do like Lucille?"

"Adore her," I said. "I think it's the Brooklynese accent in conjunction with her face that knocks me out . . . Carl!" I cried, "I just remembered! I *do* know someone who saw both me and my phony uncle together! The doorman at the apartment building! The man at the apartment saw me downstairs to the lobby when he sent me off to play with charge accounts. The doorman saw him!"

"How come you never mentioned it before this?" asked Carl.

"I'd forgotten," I explained. "How much do you think of a doorman at an apartment house? But thinking of Lucille's accent reminded me. The doorman had the same accent. He referred to my aunt and uncle as the BOIN-ards."

"Now, that's the first real break we've had, Doris," said Carl, giving my hand a squeeze. "Good thing you met Lucille, then."

"And that I'm an out-of-towner," I added. "A New Yorker probably wouldn't have noticed the accents. And speaking of accents, my friend, what was that business you gave Selim Bakka about not speaking Japanese? That wasn't Spanish you were rattling off with Lucille."

Carl smiled sheepishly. "I didn't say I can't speak Japanese. I just *said* I can't speak Japanese. That's different. You see, I wanted information from Bakka. If I'd allowed him to sidetrack me with a courtesy like speaking Japanese, I'd have lost my edge in questioning him. Don't you see? He'd have been one up on me."

"I guess . . ."

"Really," Carl continued, "it's something I learned from Professor Swersky at law school. Interrogation, whether on the witness stand or as we did with Bakka, is like a chess game. The second you're not advancing, you're losing ground. If I'd accepted Bakka's courtesy, I would have owed him one. And courtesy has little to do with getting information from a reticent witness."

I shook my head in wonder. "You're some piece of work, Mr. Suzuki," I said. "I think you'll be quite a lawyer when you get your sheepskin."

"Not good enough to trade shots with a career diplomat," Carl said ruefully. "He played me like a pinball machine. This whole expedition to see Maloney for instance. Bakka dropped the Pan-Am reference and off we went, like a couple of suckers."

"But we found out that somebody fitting the description of the Bernards got on the plane," I said.

"Which isn't too much more than what we knew at the Pan-Am office before we went downtown," Carl snorted. "No, Doris, we were had."

We got off the subway and walked east on 79th Street. In a few blocks we were once again at the point where this whole adventure had begun. It seemed amazing that it had all happened in the past twenty-four hours.

"The lobby is empty, Doris," Carl said. "Let's hope this doorman isn't off on Sundays."

We went into the ornate lobby of 820 East 79th Street. The old doorman was nowhere in view.

"He may be at the service elevator," Carl said, indicating a sign that read: *To Service Elevator.* "Let's check."

We walked down a long corridor, and just then, the elevator for deliveries opened its door and a man in a doorman's uniform got out. It wasn't the old man I'd seen yesterday. But Carl and I both recognized him immediately. It was the biggish black man who had followed us last night! He saw us, too. I saw the recognition in his face. Carl and I did an abrupt 180-degree turn and headed for the lobby again. The black doorman called after us, "Wait!" Fat chance!

We quickstepped out of the lobby and into the street. We reached the curbside, where the canopy from the building met the street line. As we did, a long, black Cadillac limousine pulled up in front and neatly blocked our way. A window on the passenger side rolled down silkily. I did a double take. The man looking out the car window was William Maloney, our airline clerk! And he didn't sound at all effeminate when he said, "Get in. Both of you."

We obeyed, not because Maloney was suddenly sounding so butch, but because he had a convincing argument. It was a very nasty-looking automatic pistol, aimed straight at my chest!

6

Not So Secret Agents

"I said 'Get in,' " Maloney repeated. "And don't even *think* of anything cute, Suzuki. This is aimed at Miss Fein."

"And this is aimed at your back," added the black "doorman" who had come up behind us. I glanced over my shoulder and saw he had his hand in his jacket pocket. I could see an outline of something that could have been another pistol. Carl shrugged his shoulders and said, "Okay. Just put that thing away."

The back passenger door opened, and I went to step inside. A hand reached out and grabbed my forearm. I was roughly pulled into the back of the car. A huge black man I'd never seen before was at the other end of the hand that grabbed me. As I unceremoniously plunked into the seat, Carl, pushed from behind, tumbled almost on top of me. The "doorman" followed us into the Cadillac. The car pulled away from the curb and headed west on 79th Street, then south on Second Avenue.

There was some wriggling around as the "doorman" took Carl's police revolver, then, despite our attempts to find out what was going on, we rode in stony silence until we pulled up in front of a commercial loft building at 39th Street and Second Avenue.

There were a number of small painted signs alongside the doorway of the loft building, each naming a tenant. *All-Africa Imports, D. N. Trading Company, Simba Ltd.,* and *Bey International Ltd.* The man in the doorman's uniform got out first and opened the street level door with a key from the bulky ring he kept in his uniform jacket pocket. The giant black man in the back seat of the Caddie growled, "Out!" We outed, with one man before us and another behind us, and with Maloney bringing up the rear. We climbed a rickety flight of stairs to the third floor of the four-story building. The "doorman" used his key ring again and opened a door marked *Simba Ltd.* It was one of those steel fire doors with the lock and keyhole in its center.

"What's this about?" I asked of anyone who might answer.

"Soon enough, Miss Fein," said Maloney from behind us. "You'll find out soon enough."

He remained in the corridor while we entered and found ourselves in an office reception area, decorated in a fashion not unlike the Dakaman offices at the UN. The effect was contemporary, but unmistakably African in tone. The "doorman" reached across the empty desk and pushed an intercom button. "We have the two of them, sir," he said. A buzzer sounded and the door separating the reception area from what I supposed was an inner office swung open. I was shoved gently from behind, and with Carl behind me, entered the inner office.

I couldn't see a thing. There were super-bright floodlights, the sort photographers use, aimed directly at the entrance to the office. I could vaguely make out a shape seated at the desk. I could also see two chairs, hard, straight-backed wooden ones, facing the desk.

A voice behind me, probably the big black man's, said, "Sit down." For emphasis, a hand the size of a country ham was placed on my shoulder. I nearly sank to my knees. I looked over and saw Carl being similarly muscled into the other chair. For the first time, the figure behind the desk spoke. I expected a foreign accent, I don't know why. Maybe the John Le Carré and Eric Ambler novels I've read. But this voice was all-American and had a midwestern twang that matched my friend Harry Grubb's. Harry is from Chicago.

"You two are a colossal pain in the butt, did you know that?" said the man in shadows. I didn't think the question was anything but rhetorical, and stayed silent. Not Carl.

"And all of you are bound for a Federal slammer," Carl said, in an official sort of tone I'd never heard him use before. "Kidnapping, violation of the Sullivan law, and a number of other offenses it'd take too long to list."

"Please, please, Mr. Suzuki," said the man in shadows, "spare me your outrage. The next thing, you'll

73

be saying 'You won't get away with this.' And obviously, we have got away with it. And more, if you don't do as you're told."

"What . . . ?" Carl began.

"Oh, really," said the voice wearily, "were you going to ask 'What's going on?' I'd expect more of a nominal professional, Suzuki. What's going on is our business, and as you two seem incapable of keeping your noses out of it, we have simply removed you from the scene. Taken you out, in a sporting sense. But don't think you can't be taken out in a literal sense. There's too much at stake for a couple of bumbling, fumble-thumbed amateurs to go messing in."

"Who are you people?" I asked, finding my tongue.

"None of your business. For what it's worth, consider us the Good Guys. We wear the white hats. Our problem is what to do with you two. But from here on out, I ask the questions, you answer them."

"I wish someone would answer just one more," I said. "It's very important."

"Very well," said the voice, much put-upon, "what is it?"

"Where's the Ladies' Room?" I asked. "I'm about to have an accident!"

"Take her," said the man in shadows to someone behind me. I felt that huge hand on my shoulder again. I got up and turned toward the door. As I did so, Carl reached over and grabbed my arm. In a split second, he'd spun me around, and I was thumped hard onto the floor. Fortunately, where I landed was well padded.

Then Carl erupted like a volcano! He moved in on the two black men guarding us. They no longer had their pistols drawn, and the "doorman" was scrambling madly for his jacket. Although he was easily three inches taller than Carl, (and who knows how much heavier), Carl moved in. He stood on one foot and seemed to launch himself into the air. His other foot connected with the bigger man's head with an audible snap. The "doorman" reeled.

While the "doorman" was off-balance, Carl appeared to dance toward the huge man remaining on his feet. With a savage cry, Carl launched himself into the air, and sailed feet first toward the giant black man!

Now I've seen a lot of Kung-Fu films. They're not to my taste. But Larry Small is crazy about them. And going out with Larry, if there's no rock concert or film of one within fifty miles, we end up at a Kung-Fu movie. For a while there, I couldn't look a bowl of rice in the eye! So when Carl Suzuki leaped through the air feet first at the giant black man, I expected what I'd seen in films. He'd nearly kick this giant's head off, right? Wrong.

The giant took some sort of sidestep and *caught* Carl in midair, as though he were a bean bag a child had tossed at him. He grabbed Carl by the crotch and shoulder and threw him across the room! That's right, threw him. Carl hit the wall with his shoulders, and the back of his head rapped the wall with a hollow *thunk*. He slid down the rest of the way and lay still. I couldn't help it, I let out a shriek you could have heard in Santa Amelia. I also wet my pants at the same time. Embarrassing to admit, but as I said, I already was in dire straits before the Kung-Fu-ing began. And though it galls me to set it down, I began to cry. You see, I thought that Carl was dead. I looked up from the floor at the gigantic black man. From that angle he looked like a fleshy black Sequoia tree. He leaned over and reached for me, and I must have squeaked like a rabbit. I had visions of being torn limb from limb, this monster playing she-loves-me, she-loves-me-not with my arms and legs. I was taken back when he smiled. Oh, my Lord, I thought. He *enjoys* this sort of thing! I knew how Fay Wray in *King Kong* must have felt at that moment. But incredibly, he only offered an outstretched hand and helped me to my feet. He guided me back to the chair I'd been sitting in. I wouldn't take the seat. I couldn't. My entire backside was wet, and I didn't want to compound matters by sitting. I was red as a tomato, I'm sure. Just then, Carl stirred, groaned and rolled over!

I rushed to his side and cradled his head in my arms. He opened his eyes then and actually grinned at me. "This is as close as I've gotten to you since we met."

I couldn't help it, the relief of tension I guess, but I broke into hysterical laughter. And held him tight against me and kissed him.

"Are you quite finished with hysteria, mock heroics and romance?" asked the acid-etched voice from the shadows. I glanced over. The man in shadow hadn't even stood up during the scuffle. He must have been very sure of the big black man's ability to subdue Carl. And his confidence had been more than justified.

"Put Mr. Martial Arts back in his chair, Bosler," he said. "And you, Miss Fein. I don't know if you need the W.C. or a change of clothing." I could see him press a button on his desk. His hands were visible in the spill from the floodlights, but the rest of him remained in shadows.

The door opened behind us. I craned my neck around and got a new attack of goosebumps. For entering the room was one of the beautiful near-twins from the Dakaman legation office. When she spoke, I recognized her as Selim Bakka's secretary.

"Please come with me, *Mademoiselle* Fein," she said. After all that had happened, I didn't resist. I followed meekly as she led me from the office. As I left, I could hear the voice of the man in the shadows say, "Now, Suzuki, let's review what you do and don't know about all this." As the door closed, I heard Carl's voice say, "Sit on it, you———!" I couldn't admire the word, but his choice was apt.

The secretary led me down the outside hall, where I noted William Maloney on guard, and into another office door marked *Employees Only*. She turned the knob on the door and showed me into an office that was the twin of the one next door. Except that stacked in a neat pile was all my luggage from the Plaza.

"There is a W.C. through that door," the secretary said, indicating an entrance. "You will leave the door open while you use it. You may also change your clothing, if you like."

"I like," I said. "In fact, I don't need the bath-room, except for some soap and water." It was mortifying, but I had to clean up and change in front of that woman. Once I'd finished, I was escorted back to the office with the bright lights. But when we returned, Carl wasn't there! I was guided to one of the hard wooden chairs, and the man in the shadows began abruptly.

"Now, Ms. Fein, we would like to know just what you think you've been doing for the past twenty-four hours."

"I'm not saying a word until I see Carl Suzuki," I said firmly. "What have you done with him?"

"He's just fine, lady," said the man in shadows. "And you haven't answered my question."

"I didn't think you really wanted an answer," I snapped. "And I won't say anything until I see and talk with Carl."

"You are in no position to make demands, Ms. Fein," said the man in shadow.

"Neither are you," I countered. "If there's anything you want to know, it must be important to you. Further, if you're the 'Good Guys' as you so quaintly put it, you aren't going to kill me if I don't cooperate. So, no chitchat until I see Carl, alive and well."

"This is getting out of hand," sighed the man in shadows. He reached into the pool of light atop his desk and pressed a button. The room lights went on, and I found myself facing a man about fifty years of age. He was in shirtsleeves and had a jacket draped over the back of the chair in which he sat. He was a bit paunchy and his hair was thinning. He had alert brown eyes that, at the time, were virtually crackling with anger. He savagely punched at his desk intercom. "Bring in the cop," he growled.

A door behind him, one I hadn't seen when the lights were in my eyes, opened. In walked the giant black man, and alongside him, looking strangely sheepish, was Carl. The middle-aged white man behind the desk waved Carl to the unoccupied chair beside me and said wearily, "All right, Suzuki, tell her all about it."

Carl sat down and reached over and took my hand. "It's all been a horrendous mistake, Doris," he began. "These men here are agents of Dakaman Intelligence, working with an American agency called the Information Gathering Organization. The IGO, for short . . . "

"But who? . . . " I started, but Carl gave my hand a squeeze and continued.

"They haven't been after us at all, Doris," Carl continued. "They have had you under protective surveillance since you showed at the 79th Street apartment."

"Then I *was* being followed at the stores!" I exclaimed. "I *knew* I felt something wrong."

"We can't outthink intuition, I'm afraid," interjected the man at the desk.

"But they outthought me, every step of the way," Carl added. "I was right. Selim Bakka was in on it. That's how we were steered to the Village. We were supposed to accept Maloney's tale that your aunt and uncle got on the flight to Dakama. Once we bought that, the IGO was free to pursue their plans without us interfering."

"What plans? What in the world is all this about?"

"We have to backtrack to when you arrived to explain that," said the man at the desk. "Hours before you arrived, the fighting broke out in Dakama. The uprising there was timed to coincide with some terrorist activity here in New York. By some fluke, a terrorist attempt to kidnap your uncle was aborted. He fought them off. However, in the scuffle, your aunt was seriously injured."

"Is she . . . ?" I asked.

"No, she's recovering in a U. S. naval hospital not

far from the city," said the middle-aged man. "But so far as the terrorists are concerned, she's out of the country. In Dakama, with your uncle."

"So Uncle Claude *is* in Dakama then," I said.

"Wrong again, Doris," Carl said. "He's right here."

"Where?" I said, looking around.

"He means right here in New York City," said the middle-aged man. "He's in hiding, under heavy guard."

"You stumbled into things coming here a day too soon," Carl said. "A telegram was sent to Santa Amelia, telling you not to come. They also telephoned, but there was no one at your home, just your father's answering service saying that he was at a convention in Hawaii. Your telegram saying that you were arriving a day early came after you'd left for your shopping tour."

"Then who was that I met at the apartment?" I asked, my mind reeling.

"That was your Uncle Claude, Doris," said Carl.

"But the beard!" I exclaimed. "What about his beard?"

"We had two decoys get on the late flight to Dakama, Ms. Fein," said the middle-aged man. "And in view of the danger to Mr. Bernard, we had him change his appearance as much as possible. Shaving the beard was the easy part. It changes a man's looks immensely."

"The idea was to have the terrorists think your aunt and uncle were on a plane for Dakama, and remove the threat to their persons," Carl added.

"But then *I* arrived," I said.

"Exactly," said the middle-aged man. "And you've been a flying pain in the coccyx ever since. You saw your uncle without his beard. We figured it wouldn't matter too much. And that you'd butt out of this entire affair."

"I would have, if it hadn't been for that phony letter," I said.

"I know, I know," said the man wearily. "We even took the letter from your room. That left-handed writing thing was a bad slip."

"But that just made me more suspicious," I said. "That's why Carl and I went to the UN. To find out the truth."

"Your quest for the truth, Ms. Fein, is why we're all here now," said the portly man. "When you and Suzuki went to the UN, we nearly had a hernia! We couldn't warn Selim Bakka that you'd seen Bernard clean-shaven. The lines were all tied up. But Bakka's a cool customer. He gave you the official scenario that the Bernards had left the country, despite the fact he knew something had gone wrong. That's a trained diplomat for you. They're able to look you straight in the eye and lie like troupers. Even when it's embarrassing."

"Surely he knew I'd check out the airline clerk," said Carl.

"Of course he did," said the man behind the desk. "But when he left you to get Bernard's personnel folder, he called us. Told us that our scenario was not playing as planned. We immediately substituted Maloney for the actual Pan-Am airline clerk. I told you he's a real pro.

"It then became our problem to either isolate you or pick you up. But we couldn't get Ms. Fein away from crowds, or you, once she picked you up."

"I picked *her* up," Carl put in.

"Nobody picked me up," I said firmly. "Any relationship with Carl Suzuki was instituted by me."

"I have no time for your love life, Ms. Fein," said the man behind the desk, "nor any face-saving details as to how you two got together. The point is this. You were wandering about, disrupting our stake-out of the apartment. And we had to be careful about how we picked you up. You were in the company of an armed policeman. For the longest time, we didn't know who the hell Suzuki was. We thought you picked him up in the bar at Trader Vic's."

"Thanks a lot," I said.

"No reflection on your morality, Ms. Fein," said the middle-aged man. "The way you conduct your sex life is none of our affair. Our concern is national and international security. But getting back to Suzuki, we had a rough few hours.

"As you may or may not know, we believe the Dakaman uprising is being bankrolled by a nation I'm not at liberty to mention. We thought Suzuki was one of theirs. What scared us most was that he was armed. Our shadow spotted his pistol right away."

Carl took over the narrative then: "They had one agent tail us, while another checked me out at the poolroom. Luckily, I'm known there. The owner knows I'm a cop. But the second tail had no way of knowing that. He followed us all the way through Central Park. Ready to kill me, if need be. They ought to give those guys two-way radios. I could have been rubbed out by mistake!"

"Whew!" I remarked.

"How do you think *I* feel?" Carl grinned. "If I'd

made a move to kiss you in the park, I'd have been cross-ventilated with a .38 before I knew what hit me."

"Once we knew Suzuki was a policeman, we contacted his superiors to have him called off; tell him to butt out," said the man at the desk. "But love conquers all, evidently. Suzuki wouldn't stay in one place long enough to get a phone call from the precinct. He's been on you like a coat of paint."

I must have blushed. I felt my face grow warm. Bless Carl. He quipped, "You mean like a coat of Japan lacquer."

"Spare me your Oriental wit, Suzuki," said the man. "You've been enough trouble as it is. We've wanted to pick up Ms. Fein and get her some place safe since yesterday. The problem was how to get her quietly and discreetly. Knowing you were armed and suspicious, we were afraid somebody might get hurt. It was just lucky for us that, after you left the Japanese restaurant downtown, you blundered into our stake-out at Bernard's apartment building. Our team from down town was just pulling up to the building when you showed up. So we took the chance on snatching you there on the street. Luckily, neither of you were hurt."

"To say nothing of your agents," I put in. "I'll bet the man Carl kicked has more than a headache right now."

"It's part of his job," said the man, matter of factly. "And a drop-kick from an amateur doesn't take out an IGO agent, lady. Bosler is just fine. The hardest part was subduing Suzuki without Habib here," he indicated the giant black man, "tearing him limb from limb. Habib is Dakaman Security, trained more to kill than subdue. Suzuki was lucky."

I turned around in my chair and looked at Habib. I shuddered when he gave me a grin a crocodile would have envied. "My apologies, *mam'selle*," he said. "I didn't mean to damage your *amant*. And it's *Major* Habib. Dakaman Foreign Intelligence." Habib had a surprisingly pleasant tenor speaking voice. It sounded incongruous coming from a man of his bulk. His accent was French, but not *charmant*, like Uncle Claude's or Selim Bakka's.

"Mr. Suzuki is not my lover, Major," I said stiffly. Habib gave a very Gallic shrug, as if to say he knew better. "As you wish, *Mademoiselle*," he said.

"If you don't mind," said the middle-aged man heavily, "I'd like to get back to the problem at hand. And it's a serious one. You, Ms. Fein, have been spotted by the terrorists and are now a potential target, with your relatives safely out of the way."

"Spotted?" I asked.

"The Hispanic type I spotted on the subway was one of theirs, not ours," Carl explained. "And we didn't shake him so easily. He saw Bosler following us and took off." Carl shook his head.

"I haven't been crafty or swift through this whole affair," Carl said. "I've been very, very lucky. We both have, Doris."

"Admission of one's ignorance is the first step toward knowledge," said Major Habib from behind us.

"An old Dakaman proverb, Major?" said the man at the desk.

"No, Confucius," replied the giant. "And speaking of our new-found brothers at the UN, what are we to do with Ms. Fein?"

"I'm coming to that, Major," said the middle-aged man. He looked me straight in the eye. "I have a proposition for you, Ms. Fein. It may be dangerous, though."

"You may call me Doris," I said coolly, "if I can call you something other than 'hey you'."

"My name is Case. George T. Case. I'm with the IGO, as Suzuki told you. It was our intent to keep you under wraps and substitute one of our agents for you. But now that you've been seen, we're stuck with you. We have two choices. We can keep you under guard — with your Uncle Claude. But that would tip the terrorists that we know what they're doing."

"What's the second choice?" I asked, but I had an idea what the answer was going to be. And I was right.

"If you'll cooperate," said George Case, "we'd like you to return to the Plaza and have a tourist-type vacation in New York. Of course, you'll be under constant surveillance. By personal observation, and electronically as well. The idea is that we want to watch and see who's watching you. At present, we haven't a glimmering as to where the terrorists are based. The two who made the attempt on your aunt and uncle are both dead. We traced them, naturally. Couple of American hoods, the equivalent of throwaways to the terrorists. And as the saying goes, 'Dead men don't talk.' All we have is a pair of corpses."

"I'm against this, Doris," said Carl.

"We duly noted your objections earlier, Suzuki," said Case. "You don't enter into this. We haven't discussed the trouble you may be in with the NYPD about operating outside your jurisdiction. To say nothing of playing Charlie Chan with Ms. Fein, here."

I saw the anger leap to Carl's face for a split second, then his face became impassive as a mask. I couldn't be quiet. "Charlie Chan is a Chinese detective, Mr. Case. Carl is an American of Japanese descent. And I think you owe him an apology."

"Deliver me," said Case, gazing at the ceiling. "For your information, Ms. Fein, I was not slurring Suzuki racially. And if it comes to that, you ought to read a Charlie Chan novel. Chan was an American, too. He worked for the Honolulu Police Department."

Case had me there. I've never read a Charlie Chan novel. I've only seen the Grade-B pictures on TV. I felt distinctly uncomfortable. But Carl gave me a quick smile that let me know he understood what I meant to say. Case continued.

"I have already arranged for Suzuki to be detached from regular duty on the NYPD. He'll be with you constantly. I trust that won't bother you too much, Ms. Fein?"

If Case was seeking to embarrass me, I wasn't about to give him that satisfaction. "I think that would be delightful," I said, and noted Carl's expression of approval.

"Good, good," said Case impatiently. "Now, all you have to do, Ms. Fein, is see the sights with Suzuki here. As soon as we spot anyone tailing you, we'll have a lead to work on; perhaps, if we're lucky, a regular member of the terrorist organization we can pick up. Then we'll sweat the information out of him."

"Or her," I interjected.

"Or her," Case agreed. "Here," he said, reaching into his desk drawer. "We want you to wear this," He took out a black velvet box, which he opened. It contained a rather oversized *mezuzah*. It was gold and as I felt the heft of it, rather heavy for a necklace.

"It has a beeper built into it. It gives off a constant radio signal that we . . . "

"I've read a few books, Mr. Case," I said. "I know what it does."

"Good, then I needn't explain any further. Will you cooperate?"

I took a deep breath. I could see Carl was concerned. He couldn't speak; I knew that. And I'm sure he didn't want me to do this. But I'd be darned if I was going to be swept under the rug and protected like a simpering ingenue. "I'll do it," I said.

For the first time since I'd seen his face, George Case smiled. It wasn't a pleasant sight. He had crooked teeth and they were badly stained from smoking, I'd guess. "That's just great, Ms. Fein," he said. Then he reached into his desk and came up with some papers. "Read these and sign all four copies," he said.

"What is this?" I asked.

"Forms. They make you a temporary agent of the IGO. It simplifies matters."

"He's saying that if anything happens to you, Doris, the IGO is off the hook for involving a civilian in all this," put in Carl heatedly. "Don't you see? You won't be that safe at all! And that beeper is a toy, nothing more. In Manhattan, with all the steel structures and interference, it's useless. It's just designed to make you feel safer!"

87

I looked over the forms. They were in legalese. I would have to hire a lawyer to figure them out. But I did note one thing. It made me a paid agent of the IGO. I turned to Case and said, "I hate to sound crass, Mr. Case, but this form mentions pay."

"Yes, it does," said Case resignedly. "It classifies you as a Rank three agent. You make twenty-thousand dollars a year."

"When's payday?" I asked.

7

Enter: Harry and Larry

On the way back to the Plaza in the cab with Carl, the gravity of what I'd committed myself to sank in on me. I recalled what I'd read in a novel somewhere. The gist of it was that when one plays at adult games, bear in mind that it's not make-believe. The stakes are high, and the games is for keeps. And if you get into trouble, don't look for the Queen's Messenger to arrive with a reprieve. Because the Queen's Messenger never arrives in real life. I mentioned this to Carl.

"That's Bertolt Brecht," he said. "The reference is from *The Threepenny Opera*. And it's something you should have thought of before you signed those papers for George Case."

"You're right!" I said. "It *is* from that show. My folks have the original cast album. 'Mack the Knife' is from that show. They saw it here in New York on their honeymoon. When they're feeling romantic, they play it on the stereo. Even now."

"I saw it, too," Carl said. "It ran practically forever here in New York. I think I was eighteen when I saw it. And you would have been . . . "

"All of about ten years old," I finished. "You know, Carl, that's the funniest thing. I don't know how old you are."

"I'll be twenty-nine years old on October 23rd of this year," he said.

"A Scorpio," I said. "Is it true what they say about Scorpios?"

"I don't know," Carl said. "I don't follow astrology. Though many Japanese do. What do they say about Scorpios?"

"They say Scorpios are very sexy people," I replied.

"Sounds like me," said Carl, smiling. Then he put his arms around me and kissed me. I kissed back, hard. By the time we reached midtown Manhattan, we were more than familiar. I kept glancing at the back of the cab driver's head. If he was spying through the rearview mirror, he didn't let on. I mentioned it to Carl. He only laughed.

"You'd have to do a lot more than some innocent necking to get a New York cabbie's attention, Doris," he said. "Some of the things that go on in the backs of cabs would amaze you."

"You can say that again, buddy," said the driver, who evidently hadn't missed a thing. "It's all the same to me, so long as they pay the fare."

"Uh, thank you for the information," Carl said to the driver. We both moved a bit farther apart on the back seat. But it started me thinking. Here I was, alone in New York City with an extremely attractive man. And a man who thought I had a great bod, which was a new experience for me. I believe I've already mentioned what the Southern California standards of beauty are. And Carl obviously liked more than my form. We liked the same things, the same books; enjoyed each other's company. It all fitted so right. And now we were on our way to *my* suite at the Plaza. That is, if the IGO had reinstated my room and got my luggage back there. I realized I just might be facing a moment of truth, sexually.

I have to say it. I'm a virgin. Not exactly for lack of opportunity. Larry Small and I have been hot and heavy at times. At least since the Danny Breckinridge episode took place. But at the time I was in the cab with Carl, Santa Amelia seemed very far away. And there was no one watching me, keeping score or tabs on what I did. No one except the IGO and the terrorists. And from what Major Habib had said, they assumed Carl and I were already lovers. I looked over at Carl. He was all attention, and the gaze he was according me had little to do with literary interest.

I knew that I'd soon have to make a decision. A few things troubled me, though. The first was my parents. They trusted me not to get myself involved in anything I couldn't handle. Another was my relationship with Larry. True, he'd never know what happened in New York unless I told him. And then, only if anything *did* happen with Carl and me. Also, there was the fear of getting myself pregnant. Well, not by myself, exactly. I had nothing for prevention. I didn't expect I'd need it. Mom and I talked about it, and she even offered to set up an appointment with her gynecologist. I think we were both embarrassed by our conversation. So we left the matter up in the air. I was beginning to think I'd have cause to regret it now.

"I'm a Taurus," I volunteered as we pulled up in front of the hotel.

"What do they say about Tauruses?" Carl asked.

"They say we're very stubborn, aggressive and when we see what we want, we go after it," I said as we walked into the lobby.

"And have you seen anything you want?" Carl asked. I think that's the point at which I had my mind made up. "Yes, I have," I answered. Then I nearly fell down in shock.

I wasn't sure I could believe my eyes. But there's no mistaking a man who looks like that. He had his back mostly toward me, but I could see his face in profile. He was a very old man, and quite tall. Six feet three inches and thin and erect as a flagpole for all his years. His full head of hair was snowy white and worn in the style that judges and lawmakers used to affect. His hair matched his full beard in color. He was wearing an old-style three-piece suit, a dark blue pinstripe, with a wing collar and narrow bow tie. He was so out of fashion, he'd come back into being chic. If I still had any doubts, they were resolved a second later, when he was joined by a young man of about eighteen, medium height, with dark hair and eyes. The eyes had a worried look, and he walked like a little boy reluctantly going to school. Both of them spotted me at the same time. I realized that I was arm in arm with Carl Suzuki, and although it couldn't have mattered less, I disengaged.

"Doris!" called the old man from across the lobby. We went over and joined them. Before anyone had a chance to talk, I said, "Carl Suzuki, these are my friends Larry Small and Harry Grubb." Then the talking began all at once. Larry didn't wait for a handshake.

"Dee, we were going crazy with worry," Larry said. "I called your aunt and uncle to see how you were, and there was no answer. I called all the hotels I could and finally tried this one, when I remembered you mentioned it. They told me you'd been here, but you checked out with no forwarding address. I didn't know what to do . . . "

"My young friend has few manners, sir," said Harry Grubb to Carl. "I'm delighted to meet any friend of Doris. My friends call me Harry." He extended his hand to Carl, who was openly confused about what was going on. To tell the truth, so was I. I was also feeling inexplicably guilty for a girl who hadn't done anything. Yet.

"Doris told me a lot about you, Harry," Carl said, shaking Grubb's hand. "But I never expected to meet you. Or not quite so soon."

"I figured that," Larry put in. He was virtually glaring at Carl. "Hi, Carl. Pleasedtameetchyou," Larry mumbled. But the fact was obvious Larry was far from pleased. I'm sure he saw the way Carl and I were looking at each other just a few seconds earlier. Or had he? Was I so bound up in feeling guilty about what I didn't do, that it was coloring my judgment?

"I must say that I'm pleased to see you relatively intact, Doris," Harry said. "It must have been contagious hysteria that brought me here. When Lawrence first came to me with his tale of supposed tragedy, I was skeptical. But I'd read and heard the news about the Dakaman revolution. And as you'd told me your uncle was with the Dakaman legation, I was a bit concerned."

"And there's no answer at your uncle's place," Larry put in. "So far as I knew, that's where you were staying."

"Oh, Larry," I said, "I told you if anything went wrong, I'd probably be staying at the Plaza."

"A fact he relayed to me, Doris," Grubb said. "But when I first telephoned this hotel, you were a checked-in guest. I told Lawrence then that you were probably out seeing the town. We tried to reach you most of Sunday, but to no avail. Then, this afternoon when we called, we were told that you'd checked out, leaving no forwarding address."

"I called at one o'clock in the morning and got no answer," Larry said. "That's one A.M. *your* time, Dee." He was staring pointedly at Carl. "I suppose you were busy," he added.

"Not awfully busy," Carl said easily. "We were out shooting pool. Doris is a great player."

"I know," Larry Small said. "I just didn't know what game she was playing, that's all. I think I know now, and I feel like a fool."

Larry's meaning was plain. But if anyone felt the fool, it was I. I hadn't told Carl about Larry. Why should I have? It was a subject that just hadn't come up. So very much had happened, and at such a furious pace, Carl and I hadn't discussed any attachments I might have had at home, emotionally. True

94

when we'd first met, there was both time and opportunity, but at that point, I wasn't personally involved with Carl. No point to it then, and no chance for it later. But my silence was about to cost me dearly. Carl was confused and, I think, getting angry. Larry was confused, angry, and coming to a dead wrong conclusion. Bless Harry Grubb. The awkwardness was so heavy in the air, you could have chewed it. Grubb broke the spell.

"Feeling the fool simply makes you a member of a very large, unexclusive club, Lawrence," he twanged in his midwestern accent. "If I had a dime for each time in my life that I felt like a fool, I'd be a very rich man. Come to think of it, I *am* a very rich man. Which means I can afford to take us all to dinner. I don't fancy standing about in this lobby airing griefs and explanations."

"I'm not hungry," Larry Small said, not taking his eyes off Carl.

"Well, I am," Harry Grubb said. "You Lawrence, have a stomach like a shark. You actually ate that abomination the airline called lunch. I, in the spirit of gastronomical survival, opted to wait until we reached New York. I shall wait no longer. Any takers for a late dinner?" Harry Grubb took out a beautiful old gold pocket watch and checked the time. "It's eight-thirty in the evening E.D. Time, and five-thirty without lunch inside my stomach."

"Are you checked in here at the Plaza?" I asked Harry Grubb.

"Alas, no," Grubb replied. "There seems to be some sort of convention in town. There always is. I couldn't get a suite at this hotel or any of the others

I usually stop at. I had to take space at the Hilton on Fifty-fourth Street and Sixth Avenue. But I won't spend any more time here without a decent meal. If you'll allow me a moment to find a pay phone, I'll reserve for us at a little place I know."

Harry went off to a nearby pay telephone and left me alone with Carl and Larry. We spent a wretchedly uncomfortable five minutes of granite silence until Harry Grubb returned.

I was relieved to see Harry come back across the lobby in that strange walk of his. He's so tall and thin, and he takes great strides. Looks sort of like a military stork.

"All set, young folks," Harry said, grinning and exposing his huge, crooked teeth. "All we need now is a taxicab that can accommodate human beings instead of sardines. I rode from the airport to the Hilton with my knees jammed up around my ears. These new cabs don't have enough room in them."

"I think we can get a five-passenger cab," Carl said. "Where are we bound for?"

"A little place I know of on East Fifty-fifth Street," Harry said airily. "But enough talk, let's get there. I could eat a horse, harness and all!" Looking like a family of ducks, we filed after Harry Grubb. Carl didn't make a move to take my arm, and Larry didn't either.

The little place Harry knew about turned out to be *La Maison Derek,* the most exclusive and expensive French restaurant in the city of New York. As the cab pulled up in front, Carl, who was seated facing me in a jump seat, whispered to me, "Dinner here costs more than I make in a month. I'm serious, Doris. I know about this place. I can't afford this."

"Relax, son," said Harry Grubb, who had overheard. "I said it was my treat. There are few joys afforded a man my age. Eating well is one of them."

The doorman opened the cab door for us and immediately was all smiles and bows. "Mr. Grubb!" he cried. "So nice to see you again. Ain't it a bit early in the year for you?"

"Unexpected trip, Albert," said Grubb, palming the man a tip. "How's business? Selling a lot of cheeseburgers here still?"

"They keep coming in," said the doorman. "Somebody's paying for the meals here." He threw open the door to the restaurant with a flourish. "I know *I* can't afford this joint."

"Always crying poverty, Albert," said Grubb as we entered. "I still think you own an apartment house on Park Avenue."

"I only wish . . . " was his reply.

La Maison Derek was a restaurant in the grand Continental manner. The decor was Louis XIV, all gilt and ivory. There were huge crystal chandeliers, mirrors, and sparkling glassware; gleaming white napery. The carpets were so plush I felt I could have worn snowshoes to traverse the small foyer that led to the dining room. An impeccably white-tied *maître d'hôtel* lit up like a neon sign when he spotted Harry Grubb. He crossed to Grubb immediately, a wide smile on his face and his arms outstretched.

"*M'sieur* Grubb!" he called, pronouncing Harry's name *Groob*. "What a delicious surprise!" he added in French.

Harry replied in French. No, I take that back. Harry replied in words, grammar and construction

97

that were French. I won't even attempt to reproduce phonetically what Harry's French sounds like. It's pure Chicago. If you've ever heard John Wayne speak Spanish in a movie, you'll get the idea. But I *could* understand what he said, and I guess when communication is paramount, any accent is acceptable.

"Armand!" Grubb said, accepting the *maître d'*s embrace. The *maître d'* being some ten inches shorter than Harry, the effect was comical enough to draw smiles from both Carl and Larry. I heaved a sigh of relief. Maybe dinner wouldn't be as deadly as I'd envisioned. "How good to see you again!" Grubb told Armand.

"Unexpected business brought me to town," Harry said. "And it wouldn't be a trip to New York without dinner at Derek's, would it?"

"A sin," Armand said. "*Non,* a capital crime! Would you like your usual table, *M'sieur* Groob?"

"*Oui,* Armand," drawled Grubb. "There will be four of us."

"*Très bien, M'sieur* Groob," the maître d' said. "This way, please?" He led us to a grand table in a corner that could have easily seated six people. As Armand led us to it, he exploded into a percussive series of tongue clicks, finger snaps, and handclaps, each one signaling various waiters and busboys. The only part of the restaurant that wasn't bowing and scraping was the physical structure itself. It must have been my imagination, but I think the crystal chandelier winked.

Carl was seated on my left, Larry on my right. Harry sat at the head of the huge oblong table, facing me.

Carl leaned over to me and whispered, "Your friend must be *some* tipper, Doris. I could have used a few customers like him when I was waiting tables at Trader Vic's." Under the table, he reached over and patted my knee. And at the same moment, Larry Small did the same thing from the other side! I was startled by the stereo effect and let out a little yip. Both Carl and Larry immediately snatched their hands back and became absorbed in an oil painting that hung on the wall behind Harry Grubb's chair. I don't know which was funnier, the simultaneous grab, or their transparent nonchalance.

You couldn't tell if Harry Grubb noticed, but a wicked grin came over his face. "Ah, Mr. Suzuki, Doris has told us your name, but little more. What is it you do here in Baghdad-on-the-Hudson?"

"Yeah, what?" added Larry pointedly.

"I'm a detective on the New York City Police Force," Carl replied. "The 141st precinct. That's over near . . . "

"Fifty-seventh Street and Park Avenue," Harry Grubb finished. "Is Bert Heller still there?"

Carl smiled widely. "No, sir. He's Assistant Commissioner now, since the election. How do you know him?"

"Met him years ago," said Harry, warming to a story. "One of our famous Chicago hit men was apprehended in New York. He'd fled here after ventilating an assistant D. A. in Cook County. I was a crime reporter for the *Chicago Tribune* in those days. I came east to cover the extradition proceedings . . . Bert was a green kid then. Just made detective, and he was so new his holster squeaked . . . "

" 'Arry, *mon cher ami!*" called a voice. We all

turned and saw a portly middle-aged man in chef's whites crossing the room. He was almost a cartoon of what a French chef looks like, from the high, fluffy crown of his *toque blanche,* the traditional chef's hat, through his neckerchief and pointy waxed mustache.

"Derek, my old friend!" twanged Harry Grubb. He unreeled a few yards of himself and warmly welcomed the chef. "Selling a lot of hotdogs, are you?"

"You wound me, 'Arry," said the little round man in mock grief. "Do I mention your basketball team?"

I should explain. Harry Grubb is the owner of our local basketball team, The Saints. They're the losingest team in their conference. I knew immediately that Derek must be a true friend of Harry Grubb. No one dares to discuss the team with him in Santa Amelia. Not even Dave Rose, the editor of Harry's newspaper, *The Record.*

"Fair enough, Derek." Grubb smiled. "You don't talk about The Saints, and I won't call for ketchup on my Beef Wellington."

The chef turned to us and spread his arms wide while shrugging his shoulders. "The man has no soul, this is obvious!" he said mournfully. "But I can see he has exquisite taste in feminine companions." The little round chef come over to me, and he actually kissed my hand! " 'Ow do you do, *mam'selle?*" he said, bowing. "I am Derek. Welcome to my 'umble establishment."

"He has all the humility of the dowager empress of China," snorted Harry Grubb.

"And *he* has all the tact of a Montmartre *mec,*" countered Derek. "He will not introduce us. He fears I shall steal you away. Which of course, I shall.

Abandon this long drink of city water, *mam'selle,*" Derek entreated of me, "I shall cook for you, and we shall make glorious love!"

"I'm afraid you're putting the bad mouth on the wrong escort, Derek." Harry Grubb grinned. "This is Ms. Doris Fein and she's with . . . " Harry savored the moment. He purposely left the sentence hanging. He watched with malicious glee as both Carl and Larry opened their mouths to claim themselves as my escort.

"I am with myself, and on vacation from California," I said in French. It was one of the phrases I'd practiced when I thought I'd be meeting some of Uncle Claude's friends from the UN. "And I'm enchanted to meet you, Derek."

I shouldn't have done it. I got a machine-gun burst of French in return. I caught about one word in four. Derek was repeating his offer to make love, with graphic embellishments over the English version. I knew it was quite naughty, but somehow, not at all offensive. But then again, in French, it even sounds charming to me when someone asks for directions to the john.

Derek said it was out of the question that anyone see a menu. He, personally, would see that we dined well. Armand would see to the dessert, and if the lowborn son of a diseased camel who masqueraded as a *sommelier* would stop stealing his money for not doing his job, a suitable number of bottles would be found.

The meal was beyond belief, terribly French, exquisitely delicious, and about two thousand calories per forkful. Naturally, there was a vintage wine with

101

every course. I was getting a bit tiddly from all the wine, so I had a Perrier water with dessert. The end course was *Crêpes à la Maison,* served *flambé* by Armand at tableside. The whole meal was a production that made *Star Wars* look like Saturday morning cartoons. I saw Larry's eyes grow wide as Armand set the crepes on fire. Our eyes met and he said, "Sure beats IHOP, don't it?" I was mortified.

All through the dinner, I'd been watching both Carl and Larry. If Carl was in unaccustomed surroundings, you'd never have known it from the way he carried it off. On the other side, Larry looked like such a . . . well, such a *boy.*

But I was glad dinner was a production. It obviated most conversation that wasn't "Ooooh!" and "Have you tasted *this?*" A temporary respite, I knew, but a welcome one. Sooner or later we were going to have to talk about me, my relationship with Carl, and what was already nagging at the back of my mind.

Harry Grubb and Larry had come storming out to New York from Santa Amelia because they were concerned about my welfare. Then, when they'd found me, I was in Carl's company and on the IGO payroll. So far as they knew, it was all a false alarm. But there was no way in the world I could explain to them what was going on.

I knew that only the truth would satisfy Larry Small. Harry Grubb, being Harry, would think what he chose to think. And I could not, being sworn to secrecy, tell anyone the truth!

I also knew that Larry didn't have the money to fly out here. It may even have cost him his job at *The Register* to take off this way. He might have borrowed the money from his mother, or Harry Grubb. I knew to lie to him would cost me our relationship. I felt doubly guilty because seeing Larry and Carl side by side, Larry was coming off a very poor second. If I lied to Larry, it would look as though I were throwing him over for Carl. And in truth, part of me wanted to do just that. In all, it was the most exquisite, dreadfully uncomfortable dinner I've ever eaten. I think the only two people who enjoyed the dinner without a care were Harry Grubb and Petunia . . .

8

The Prisoner
of the Hilton

The cab ride to Harry's hotel was as uncomfortable as the dinner had been for me. We again found a five-passenger cab, and I sat between Harry Grubb and Larry Small, facing Carl who rode a jump seat. Carl and Larry spent the ride either glancing at each other, or making desultory conversation.

But none of it bothered Harry Grubb, who kept up a running monologue on how New York City had changed for the worse, and that we all should have seen the town years ago. I was relieved when we pulled up in front of the Hilton. It's a huge hotel, larger by far than the Plaza. More like a smallish city than a hotel.

"Who's for a nightcap?" asked Harry Grubb.

I checked my watch. "Hardly a nightcap," I said. "It's only 11:30."

"You charming young people may be left to your

own devices, I'm sure," Harry Grubb said. "But I have had a full day. I have been cross-country in a jet, somehow survived a cab ride from JFK International, and eaten a magnificent dinner. I'm ready for a cigar, a brandy and a night's sleep. I was provident enough to bring some of my own cigars. They're upstairs."

"You gotta see where we're staying, Dee," Larry chimed in. "You won't believe it!"

I knew very well that Harry was trying to get back at me for bringing him east on what he deemed a false alarm. I'm sure Grubb thought I'd been off playing footsie with Carl Suzuki, and that had been the reason Larry couldn't locate me by telephone. Larry didn't just think the same thing; he was sure. Were it not for gravity of what I knew to be going on, it might have been funny. Harry wanted to stick me with both Carl and Larry.

But I wasn't about to have Harry Grubb leave me alone with Carl and Larry. "I'd love to see your rooms," I said.

"Rooms?" Larry said. "Not rooms, Dee, a whole suite!"

I smiled to myself. Larry's never been farther away from home than Los Angeles or San Diego. And he hadn't seen my suite at the Plaza. He probably thought the Hilton to be the height of elegance. Which it is, in a way. But after all, it's not the Plaza.

"We have to take two elevators," Harry Grubb said as he punched a button in the lobby elevator. The car rose to a high floor. There were several other guests in the elevator with us, which precluded conversation.

We got off at the last floor indicated, and Harry

105

led us down a corridor, past a sign on a wall that indicated: *To Tower Elevators*.

At the end of the corridor there was another elevator entrance, with a young man in a uniform standing outside it. He was smoking a cigarette, which he hastily extinguished when he saw our party coming down the hall.

"Good evening, Mr. Grubb." He smiled cheerily and took his post at the elevator controls. Without Grubb saying a word, he punched a button marked *Presidential Suite*. The doors opened onto the suite itself.

It was huge, lavish, and two floors high. It had a winding staircase that led to the upper level, and a panoramic view of the city that made me catch my breath. The appointments were impeccable, the decor, though somewhat modern/sterile in light of the Plaza, was consistent and luxurious.

Carl let out a long, low, whistle. "You do travel in style, Mr. Grubb," he said.

"Not my idea," said Harry Grubb. "I told you there was a convention in town. It's all I could get. Fortunately, I can afford this pleasure dome. Lawrence and I could rattle around in here and not see each other for days. Happily, we'll both be on our way back soon. Now that we know that Doris isn't in the *deadly* peril Lawrence thought her to be." Harry's meaning was plain. "I was possessed of the foresight to cut notches in the doorways, so I think I can find my bedroom, my suitcase, and cigars." He walked up the big, winding stairway. Trying to avoid Larry's gaze, I drifted over to the wall of windows that overlooked Central Park. Behind me, I heard Larry say, "Tell me, Carl, how did you and Doris meet?"

"Where I work," I heard Carl say. "She thought for a while that her aunt and uncle were missing. She didn't know they'd been called back to Dakama unexpectedly. She was going to file a missing persons report on them."

"And you work in Missing Persons?" Larry asked.

"Errr, no," Carl said. "I was working on my day's report when she came into the squad room . . . "

"Ahhh," said Harry Grubb, descending the staircase in a cloud of blue cigar smoke. "What a difference a good Havana cigar makes in one's postprandial outlook."

"Havanas?" asked Carl. "How do you get them? I thought that we didn't import them anymore, since Castro took over."

"We don't," said Harry Grubb, smiling. "I have a friend who labors in the diplomatic groves for a government that does have diplomatic relations with Cuba. He gets them for me. If that makes me a godless Commie, it's only by inhalation. Would you care for one, Carl?"

"No, thank you, I don't smoke," he said.

"You're not making me angry, son," said Harry Grubb. "I didn't bring that many with me. How about a brandy? The hotel has stocked the bar fully and well. They should at these prices."

Harry strolled over to a bar that would have serviced a party of fifty, easily. He walked behind it to the service area and selected a bottle. *"Martel Cordon Bleu* all right?" he asked.

"Fine with me." Carl smiled.

"I don't drink," Larry said sulkily.

"I know, Lawrence," said Harry. "That's why I offered only to Carl. And as Doris was taking Perrier after dinner, I can assume that Carl and I are the only degenerate boozers in the party."

"I changed my mind," said Larry Small, "I will have a drink."

I knew very well that Larry was showing off. He didn't want to seem like a kid in the company of men. The usual macho nonsense. Though, for the life of me, I don't understand the attitude. To my way of thinking, there's nothing particularly manly about drinking. And there is certainly nothing manly about being drunk.

Harry Grubb poured three cognacs into balloon glasses and set them on the bar. Each of the men picked up a glass. "Well, here's looking up your old address," said Harry Grubb, raising his glass. He took a sip, then picked up his cigar. But not Larry. He raised his glass and said, "Here's to finding Doris, safe and sound!" And with that, he drained the glass. The look on his face as he swallowed was almost indescribable. The closest I can come is that he appeared to have swallowed a dead mouse. That was on fire. I watched as his face turned red, his eyes watered and then he turned deathly pale. "Excuse me," he said, in a barely audible voice, and took off, almost running, for the upstairs bathroom. Harry waited until we heard the bathroom door slam and water start running. Then he threw back his head and roared with laughter. That set Carl off, and although I thought it cruel the way they were having fun at Larry's expense, I remembered the look on Larry's face, and I couldn't help it — I laughed too.

As soon as I caught my breath, I said, "I think you two are hateful! You know Larry doesn't drink,

Harry Grubb. You egged him on . . . " I had a sudden vision of Larry's face, and I broke up again. We were all giggling as Larry made his way shakily down the stairs to the lower level of the suite.

"What's wrong, son?" Harry Grubb called to him. "I hope it wasn't Derek's dinner. He'd be crushed to think his masterpiece of culinary art upset someone."

"Jet lag, I think," said Larry Small, in a squeaky voice. His eyes were all bloodshot and his skin was pale green.

"Know just what you need," said Harry Grubb maliciously. He poured another tall cognac into the glass Larry had drained moments before. "Little drink will straighten you right out!"

Larry took one look at the new drink on the bar, pivoted on his heel, and raced back up the stairs.

"Your friend isn't much for conversation, Doris," said Carl slyly.

"And you both aren't much for having a conscience between you!" I said angrily. "Harry Grubb, you are an evil man with a perverted sense of humor. And your new-found drinking buddy isn't any better. I won't stay here and have you bait Larry Small just because he isn't the big, hairy-chested supermale egos that you are. I'm going back to the Plaza. I'll speak to you in the morning!"

I strode to the elevator door and rang the bell to summon the operator. Harry and Carl saw I was genuinely upset, and both made a move toward me, just as the elevator door slid open. I was about to throw a nasty exit line at them, so I was facing away from the elevator doors as they opened. I had my mouth open to deliver the *mot juste,* when I saw the expressions on their faces. They were both about twelve feet away from me at the time. I turned to see what they were staring at.

The man in the elevator wasn't the operator who'd brought us up. He wasn't wearing a Hilton uniform. He was wearing coveralls and a menacing look. It went perfectly with the automatic rifle he had leveled at Carl and Harry Grubb. "Freeze!" commanded the man in the car. Harry and Carl froze.

The man reached out with his free hand and grabbed me by the front of my dress. I felt some of the lightweight fabric tear, as I was hauled unceremoniously into the car. I can still see the looks on Harry's and Carl's faces as the door closed.

Though the doors had closed, the man made no move to set the car in motion. He turned to me and said, "Lady, if you open your mouth, I'll shut it for good with this." He gestured with the automatic rifle cradled in his arm. "Do you understand?" I nodded, too terrified to speak. "Good," he said. "Do what you're told, and we won't have any problems." Then he started the elevator.

I prayed that there'd be someone in the corridor when the elevator stopped at the lower floor. But the hall was deserted. I was hustled to a door marked *Service,* and with the armed man behind me, we walked down ten flights of stairs. I judged it put us on the fourth or the third floor. We went through an empty banquet room, lighted only by small work lamps. In seconds, we were walking through a huge room filled with machinery. Evidently the Hilton is one of those hotels that has no basement.

I learned later that because there's so much underground wiring, subways and water mains, steam lines and gas lines in Manhattan, many big buildings have no basements. Honest. The Empire State Building itself has no basement, as such. The Hilton has its equivalent of a boiler room, with heating and air-conditioning plants on a middle floor. As we walked hurriedly through the maze of pipes, valves, and giant ductwork, I got no talk from the armed man other than "Straight ahead" or "Left here, right there." By the time we stopped in front of a door on a side corridor, I was completely disoriented.

The armed man rapped on the door. Three short, one long knock. The door opened to reveal a short, wiry black woman in a white uniform like a nurse's. I was shoved from behind and nearly stumbled into a tiny room. The wiry black woman grabbed at me, and I *did* fall. The door slammed shut, closing out the armed man. The wiry black woman quickly double-locked the door and crossed over to where I lay sprawled out. She prodded me with a foot and said, "Get up, bitch, you're not hurt."

I got to my feet and looked around me. It was a very small room, with an even tinier bathroom adjoining it. There was no furniture, save for a couch, a counter, and some restaurant chairs. The chairs were set in front of the counter. It was obviously a dressing room of some sort.

"Sit over there on the couch," ordered the wiry black woman, producing a long kitchen knife from the bathroom. "Make a funny move, and I'll spill your guts all over the room." For emphasis, she waved the razor-sharp blade under my nose. I sat.

"What's going on?" I began, but the woman waved the blade again.

111

"You're our hostage," said the black woman. "You still can get out of this alive, if you do exactly as you're told. Understand?"

"It won't work," I said. "One of the men I was with when your gorilla grabbed me is a New York cop. They'll be turning this hotel upside down in a few minutes."

"You'd better pray they don't, lady," said the woman. "The first time somebody who doesn't know the code knock comes to that door, I have orders to cut your throat." Seeing my look, she laughed. A short, nasty bark. "Don't worry about that, piglet," she said acidly. "They'll never look here. You'd have to see the plans to this hotel to even know this room exists. It used to be a dressing room when they had shows downstairs. But parts of the hotel were redesigned. And now this room is cut off from downstairs."

I ignored the piglet reference and said, "But in time, they'll check. And you won't get away. If you kill me, you'll be trapped in here, with the authorities outside the door."

"Foolish pig," she said venomously. "Do you think that matters? One life for the cause. That's all I am. And I'd gladly die, knowing I can take a money-grubbing imperialist bitch with me!" She sat down in the chair opposite me and subsided into a hateful silence.

We sat there that way for what seemed like hours. Finally, I tried to open a conversation. "But I don't understand why you should be interested in me. I'm just a tourist from California. I think you've made some mistake."

"No mistake," said the woman. "We know who

you are. You're the niece of the Dakaman Foreign Economic Secretary, Claude Bernard. Did you think we didn't know? By now, our demands are in the hands of the Dakaman legation. They will deliver Bernard to us, and we will trade you for him, at a place designated."

"You'll never get me out of the hotel to do it. I'm sure all exits are sealed by now," I said.

The woman laughed. "You're assuming they think you're still in the hotel. I'm sure your cop friends figure you're long gone by now. There wasn't time to seal off all the exits when you were snatched. There are seven public and two employee entrances to this hotel. By the time your pig friends would have called the desk, or the rest of the pigs, they'd have assumed you and your captor were long gone. No, piglet, we have you just where we want you. And we're right here, under their stupid, oppressive noses!" She laughed again.

I glanced at my watch. It had been nearly an hour since the armed man had grabbed me. As we sat in silence, I watched the hands on my watch slowly inch across the face. It was two hours before the wiry black woman spoke again. She checked her watch and said, "All right, piglet. Time we were going." She stood up and stretched; yawned luxuriously. She motioned me to stand against the wall, away from the door, while she reached inside the tiny bathroom. She hooked a cardboard box with her foot and kicked it into the center of the little room. "Open it up, and put it on," she commanded.

The box contained a white uniform, the duplicate of the one worn by the wiry woman. I took out the uniform and held it against me. "It'll fit, piglet," snarled the woman. "It's a large size. Now, hurry it up!"

I did as I was told. The uniform did fit. I looked in the mirror. I was a mess, my hair standing on end, and a big smear of eyeshadow crossed my right cheek. "Can I clean up?" I asked the woman.

"Just a minute," she snarled. She grabbed at my purse, which was on the couch. She hurriedly inspected the interior of my bag and tossed me my hairbrush. I suddenly had a brainstorm. "Can I have my hair spray too?" I asked. The woman nodded and tossed the can to me.

I took as long as I could. If what I had in mind was to work, she had to be close to me. Sure enough, her impatience began to work in my favor. Feigning clumsiness, I made another pass at my hairbrush in one hand, small can of hair spray in the other. I let the brush fall to the floor. "Pick it up," rapped the woman. I bent over, which placed me no more than three feet from her. And as I stood up, I aimed the hairspray can straight in her eyes and pressed the nozzle. I immediately jumped to one side, and a good thing I did. Even though she was blinded momentarily, the woman slashed at the air where I'd been with that long knife! I heard the hiss of the blade as it passed no more than a whisker away from my face.

I dropped the spray can and frantically looked around me. The woman was still slashing at the air. And in this tiny room, I wouldn't be hard to locate, blinded though she was. All I could see were the restaurant chairs: I picked one up, and holding it as a lion tamer in a cage does, I rammed it into her, chair legs first, and pinned her against the wall. One of the chair legs caught her squarely in the solar

114

plexus, I guess. She let out a huge *whoof* and sank to the floor.

I don't like to set this part down. I don't think of myself as a violent person. But I didn't know if the wiry woman was really unconscious, or shamming. She was on the floor between me and the door. If I passed by her to get out, she could grab me. I'd been lucky so far, but in an all-out fight, I didn't know if I could handle her. I raised the chair high over my head and brought it crashing down on her inert form.

She immediately exploded into a rush of obscenities and made random grabs and kicks in my direction. She evidently was regaining her vision from the hairspray eyebath I'd given her. I raised the chair and struck again. This time, I caught her squarely atop the head. The chair splintered, and the woman dropped like a stone. I gazed down at her and fought back the urge to vomit. Shaking all over, I gingerly stepped over her body and unlocked the door to my prison. I stuck my head out the door and peered down the outside corridor. It was empty.

I quickly raced down the passageway and to the door at its end. I pushed open the door and found myself again in the maze of pipes and machinery. I didn't know where I was or where I was going. There wasn't a soul in sight. I could have screamed my head off for help. But over the sounds of the air-conditioning plant, if that's what it was, I wouldn't have been heard. I chose an aisle among the machinery that looked likely and ran down it, toward I don't know what.

The aisle ended at two large doors with chicken-wired glass insets. Beyond them through the glass, I could see the entrances to the banquet rooms. The floors outside the doors were carpeted, not the asphalt tile of the machinery room. It was a public corridor I'd stumbled onto! I pushed halfway through the doors, and was about to race down to a bank of public elevators I spotted. As I did so, one of the doors opened, and out came a man dressed in an ambulance attendant's uniform. But I knew him immediately. Even without his automatic rifle. It was the man who had snatched me from the Presidential Suite!

9

Embarrassed
at the Bridge

I quickly turned around and went back inside the
boiler room and dashed down a side aisle of
machinery. The man from the elevator walked
by, within inches of me. I supposed he didn't
see me because he didn't expect to. So far as he
knew, I was still in that little room. Once he passed,
I made another run for the glass-paneled doors.
Fear lent impatience, and impatience bred disaster.
I glanced over my shoulder as I pushed through the
glass-paneled doors. He was standing at the back
of the machinery-filled room, his mouth agape in
surprise. The moment lasted for just a split second,
then he was in motion. After me!

I'd originally planned to take an elevator, but that
was out of the question now. I ran down the carpeted
corridor and, blessedly, I saw a sign reading: *To
Stairs.* I half ran, half tumbled down three flights. I
could hear the man from the elevator clattering

down behind me. They were uncarpeted concrete steps, with antiskid risers, and sound carried in the concrete stairwells. I tripped on the last two steps of the last flight, and charged bull-like through the door at its end.

I burst out of the door directly into the crowded lobby. I knew the man in the white uniform was right behind me, so I kept going. I doubted he'd make a fuss in a crowded lobby, but there was little doubt that he and the wiry black women were terrorists. And terrorists don't seem to care if they get caught, so long as they attain their ends. This man chasing me might very well do me in right in the center of the lobby!

I raced past a bank of house telephones. No time to stop and try to reach Harry's suite. And as the wiry woman had said, they were most likely looking for me elsewhere. I scanned faces in the lobby, hoping to spot a policeman, or one of the faces I'd seen when the IGO had brought Carl and me to the building downtown. No luck. I glanced over my shoulder. The man in white was less than twenty feet away from me. For a second, I stopped moving and looked all around.

There were windows, ceiling high, in this section of the lobby that looked out onto 54th Street. Through the glass, I saw that there was a late movie at a motion picture house across the way from the hotel, just letting out. And controlling the crowds was the most welcome sight I'd seen in New York. A big, red-faced uniformed New York City policeman! I darted through the revolving doors, with the man in ambulance attendant's uniform only feet behind me. I almost ran into the big cop's arms and panted, "Help me! That man is after me, wants to kill me!"

The cop didn't bat an eye. I guess with all that goes on daily in New York, it's as hard to startle a cop as it is a cabbie.

"What man are you talking about?" he asked boredly. And at that moment, the man in white pulled up and laid a hand on my forearm. He wasn't even out of breath, like I was.

"So glad you stopped her, officer," he said easily. "I was afraid she'd get away again."

"What is all this?" the cop asked.

I didn't wait for the man in white to say more. I jumped right in. "This man is a Dakaman terrorist," I panted. "He kidnapped me from the Presidential Suite at the Hilton. They had me locked up, but I escaped. I'm an agent of the IGO. I . . . "

I trailed off on my breathless monologue. Both the cop and the man in white were looking at me and smiling! "You see my problem, officer?" said the man in white. "She overpowered her nurse and stole the uniform. You can see her shoes aren't nurse's shoes. I was about to transfer her to the Dalewood Home. That's were she escaped from. In Dalewood, New Jersey." The man in white paused. "She's not really dangerous." He smiled. "She just has this delusion that she's a counterspy, saving our country from peril within."

"Don't you believe it!" I cried. "It's in all the papers. The uprising in Dakama. You must have seen it on TV!"

"Ah, Doris, there you are, you naughty girl!" said a voice. I spun around and found myself face to face

119

with a man of about fifty. He wore a conservative business suit, pale blue shirt, and a subdued striped tie. His hair was salt-and-pepper gray and he sported a Vandyke beard. He spoke to the man in white.

"It's all right, Wilson," he said. "I'll stay with her. You go fetch the ambulance." The man in white loped off toward the entrance to the Hilton garage, which faces onto 54th Street. Then the man with the beard turned to the policeman and took out his wallet. He handed an engraved business card to the cop.

"I'm Dr. Alex Kinsky, officer, Director of Dalewood Sanitarium. Miss Fein here has had us worried sick for hours now. We have a supervised leave program for our nondangerous patients. Miss Fein was to have seen the show at Radio City Music Hall and return to Dalewood with her nurse. We obviously . . . er, miscalculated how exciting the trip would be for her. She eluded her nurse, even stole her uniform. We've been sick with worry about Miss Fein. She's not dangerous to anyone but herself." He gave me a look like I was a kid caught in a jam jar. "Now you mustn't do things like this if you expect to get well, Doris, dear," he oiled, as the ambulance, with the man in white at the wheel, pulled up.

"This is some kind of nightmare!" I protested. "You can check out my story. I really am with the IGO!"

"Yeah," drawled the cop. "And I'm Bugs Bunny, lady." He turned to the man who called himself Dr. Kinsky. The bearded man had produced a small hypodermic needle from someplace.

"I'm afraid I'll have to sedate her, officer." He smiled apologetically. The man in white had gotten out of the ambulance and fastened a steely grip on

120

my arm. That's when I noticed the precinct number on the lapel of the cop's uniform. It read 141st precinct. That was Carl's precinct!

"Wait, please, just a second!" I entreated. "I can prove who I am. And that I'm what I say. You're from the 141st precinct. I know people there!" The cop hesitated for a second. "There's Detective Suzuki. Carl Suzuki. He's my friend. And there's a dreadful nasty detective lieutenant named . . ." I groped for the name. "Linderman!" I exclaimed triumphantly. "He's fiftyish, gray hair, overweight and has a sarcastic manner. Detective Suzuki is about thirty, and is Japanese-American."

The policeman was paying attention now! "Just a minute," he said to Dr. Kinsky. "What she's saying is true. We got an Oriental on the detective squad. I don't know him, but I seen him. And she sure knows Lt. Linderman. I think you people had better . . . "

I'll never know what he was going to say. At that second, Dr. Kinsky plunged the hypodermic right through the policeman's uniform sleeve and injected the contents. The cop turned as though stung. He made a move toward Dr. Kinsky, his hand reaching for the pistol at his side. Then a vague, dreamy look came over his face. If the man in white hadn't grabbed the cop under the arms, the officer would have fallen to the pavement. Within seconds, the ambulance driver had hustled the cop's unconscious form inside the back of the open-doored ambulance. Dr. Kinsky muscled me in after them.

The attendant laid the policeman on the bed arrangement in the ambulance. I sat with Dr. Kinsky, facing the cop's inert body. The attendant slammed the doors, and we pulled away from the curb.

"Good try, Ms. Fein," said Dr. Kinsky, as the driver turned on the siren and flashing lights. "You just may be an agent, at that. But it doesn't matter." He pulled the side curtains of the ambulance shut, obscuring us from view and regarded me with an oleaginous smile. "We've had our little difficulties, but here we are, reunited. I must ask you to remain quite still now. Unfortunately, I had to use my one shot of Demerol on this chap, here," he said, indicating the unconscious policeman. "But I must warn you, Ms. Fein," he continued, "when we cross the George Washington Bridge into New Jersey, you can cry out all you like. It will be highway driving. However, if you utter a peep, or cause the slightest disturbance before then, I will have to subdue you physically. This will entail a pressure on your windpipe until you're unconscious. It's tricky, and there's a risk of crushing the small bones there, and then you'd strangle. I wouldn't advise a fuss."

I looked at the man, and despite his easy manner, I saw in his eyes that he seemed capable of doing exactly what he said. "I'll behave," I said.

"There's a sensible girl." He smiled approvingly. "You may yet get out of all this alive. You nearly spoiled our plans, you know."

"Good!" I said.

"Now, now," he oozed. "That's not a cooperative attitude. But there isn't much you can do to stop things now. All you have accomplished with your histrionics is a small delay in our schedule. You were to have been taken out of the Hilton under sedation, once the authorities felt you were no longer on the hotel premises. But improvisation is the hallmark of a professional. When you escaped from Joanne in the

122

little room, you saved us the fuss of carrying you about on a stretcher. I had a dicey moment when you began naming names to this chap in blue, here, but all's well that ends well, as the Bard says."

"But what's . . . "

"What's this all about?" asked the bearded man. "Oh, really, Ms. Fein. Simply put, we are exchanging you for your uncle. At a place already designated. As I said, if you behave, you may get out of this affair with a whole skin."

"The IGO will be out looking for me," I said.

Dr. Kinsky threw back his head and laughed. "They certainly will. In fact, they are. We took a page from their book. A woman fitting your description has been spotted at Kennedy International. Just as a couple fitting the description of your aunt and uncle were seen boarding a flight for Dakama. Your counterspy friends are now in the process of sealing off JFK International. I wish them luck." Dr. Kinsky leaned over and checked the pulse of the unconscious policeman. "He's just fine. He'll be in dreamland for a few hours more." Kinsky checked the street, peeking through the drawn curtains. "Just about ten minutes to the bridge," he announced, like a tour guide.

"What are you getting out of this?" I asked Kinsky. "You're obviously not a Dakaman."

"I am getting the reward of having done my job well, Ms. Fein," he said. "A great deal of money. This revolutionary group from Dakama are long on courage and audacity, but they're hopeless amateurs. Being new to the revolutionary trade, they did the one sensible thing they've done so far. They hired me. In all modesty, Ms. Fein, ever since they botched the kidnap attempt on your relatives, I have been directing the operation. Quite well, I might add."

"But you're an American," I protested. "How can you sell out for money?"

"Money, Ms. Fein, is the only thing one sells out for," said Kinsky. "And you're wrong. I'm not an American. My nationality is . . . well, international, shall we say?" He took a peek out of the curtains again. "Ah, here's the bridge approach. There are no toll booths leaving the city. Please fell free to shout and scream all you like." He leaned back and regarded me with a slimy smile.

"How are you planning to get away and spend all this money?" I asked. "I know you; I've seen and can describe you . . . " I broke off suddenly. I'd realized that he had no intention of letting me go to give his description to the authorities. He'd only wanted me quiet during the ride out of New York.

"Perhaps you would have made a good agent, Ms. Fein," said Kinsky. "Yes, this is your last ride, dear." He scratched at his beard, delicately. "If you wish to remain alive for a few more hours, when we arrive at Dalewood, you will make a tape recording. The message will be that you're alive, well, and frightened. After that, a simple injection, and you will go to sleep. Peacefully. However, if we must physically persuade you, you will die in a singularly unpleasant fashion. Eddie, our driver, has a rather lurid imagination for such things. I promise you, you won't like it."

There was no answering Kinsky's remarks. He volunteered no more information, nor conversation. In a few seconds, he began to hum a little tune under his breath! I think that frightened me more than anything that had happened in the past forty hours. I tried to check out the interior of the ambulance as unobtrusively as possible. The only way out I saw was the way we'd entered. The two back doors. There was a large, swivel handle that allowed both doors of the ambulance to swing open wide. I made up my mind that if the ambulance slowed down at all, I was going to try to reach those doors and jump out. As near as I could see, there was no inside lock on the doors.

I knew I was taking a chance on being splattered all over a freeway in the process, but with certain death at the end of this ride, I figured I had nothing to lose.

"Don't bother, dear," said Kinsky, as though he'd read my mind. "You'd end up as bloody smear on the pavement. Granted you could get past me, which you can't. I'd suggest you relax and enjoy the ride to Dalewood." He peeked through the side curtains again. "Almost at the end of the bridge," he announced. "It won't be long now. We . . . "

The ambulance driver applied the brakes with a squeal. The big vehicle slewed sideways, and everything in its rear slid and tumbled. Kinsky was thrown clear across the back of the ambulance, and only by a fast dodge did I avoid his landing on top of me. The curtain he'd been holding tore away in his grasp, and I caught a glimpse of flashing red lights.

The ambulance had almost stopped, and now was swinging around in the opposite direction. It was the only chance I had, and I took it. I scrambled over the jumble in the back of the ambulance and managed to grab hold of the door handle. Kinsky had regained most of his balance and grabbed at me. He caught a good handful of the white uniform I was wearing.

They say when you're frightened near to death, a person can perform amazing feats of strength. It has to do with adrenalin pumping through the system. I can believe it. The uniform was made of sturdy fabric, but I pulled with all my might, using the door handle for leverage. With a loud rip, the entire garment pulled away from my body. With the bearded man's grip released, the door popped open, and I fell out of the back of the ambulance!

I hit the pavement of the George Washington Bridge and rolled over a few times. I felt a heavy thump as my head hit. Somehow, I regained my feet. I stood up in time to see a rare panorama.

The far end of the bridge, which was in sight, was blocked off by marked police cars, with flashers and sirens going. The ambulance was stopped and some men in civilian clothes were wrestling with the driver. Another group was running pell-mell after Kinsky, who was racing down the sidewalk that adjoins the bridge roadway. He turned momentarily, and I saw he had a pistol. He fired a shot at his pursuers, then began running again. He didn't get far. A party of men was running toward him from the opposite side of the bridge.

Kinsky saw there was no getting away. He fired the pistol again, once at the men facing him, and again, at the men behind him. When his pursuers took cover, he vaulted to the rail of the sidewalk, hundreds of feet above the Hudson River. He stood poised for a split second, balancing on the rail. Then, so help me, he turned, smiled at the two men approaching, threw them all an upright middle finger and dove over the side!

I turned and saw a group of men coming toward me. One of them was George Case! He had taken off his suit coat and was advancing toward me. It was only then that I realized I was standing in the middle of the George Washington Bridge in a set of pantyhose and my shoes! I don't wear a bra, and the weather was too warm for a slip.

I covered my breasts as best I could with my hands and arms. Case got within three feet of me, when all around me got blurry. Maybe it was the aftershock, maybe the bump I'd got on my head. I can't say. But I passed out cold.

10
Paris in the Spring?

I woke up in the back of a car, speeding through some countryside I didn't recognize. George Case was sitting next to me, and I remembered in a rush that I was wearing his suit jacket. I would have been somewhat embarrassed, but in view of my unintentional strip act on the George Washington Bridge, it didn't seem important. What did seem important was where we were going. The car we rode in was definitely not headed for Manhattan. Case saw me stirring and said, "Glad to see you with us again, Ms. Fein."

"Where are we going?" I asked fuzzily. My mouth wasn't working as well as my thought processes.

"Debriefing," answered Case, as if I should know.

"Swell," I said. "What's debriefing?"

"You spent some time with the Dakaman Terror Underground," Case said. "A lot of what you saw and heard may seem unimportant to you. Perhaps inconsequential. But what you know now may dovetail with bits of data we've accumulated."

"I see."

"And more than that," he continued, "we have to screen what data you can discuss with non-IGO cleared personnel once you're debriefed."

"You mean Larry Small and Harry Grubb?" I asked.

"That's exactly who I mean," said Case. "And your detective boyfriend, Suzuki, as well. He was acting as your bodyguard, no more. He's still a New York City cop. By the way, he didn't do such a great guarding job, either."

"No one could have anticipated what happened," I said defensively.

"The Dakaman Underground did," Case said. "They switched the site of their grab from your hotel to Grubb's, and never dropped a stitch. They may have a similar setup at the Plaza, but I doubt it."

"But where are my friends? Carl, Larry, and Harry Grubb?" I asked. "Do they know I'm safe? When can I see them?"

"Whoa, whoa!" said Case, smiling for the first time since I'd met him. "One question at a time. First, your friends know you're safe. They are currently on their way to Manhattan from Kennedy Airport. They were out there to check the identity of a woman fitting your description who was seen there."

"That was a plant, that woman who looked like me. I heard about her from Dr. Kinsky, the man who jumped off the bridge . . . "

"Save it," said Case, holding up a hand. "Once we

get to our installation in Stockholm, we'll put it all on tape."

"Stockholm?" I squeaked. "We're going to Sweden?"

"No, Stockholm, New Jersey," laughed Case. "It's about forty-five miles west of New York, in Morris County. We have a nice place on a lake. You'll love it."

"I doubt it."

"Try to love it, then," Case said. "You'll be there for twenty-four hours, minimum. We want to make sure we learn everything you saw and heard." He scratched his scalp, where he had a bald spot. "And we want to check you out medically. Our doctor on the spot said that your faint was probably due to release of tension. An afterreaction to the danger you'd been facing. But he also said there was a chance you had a mild concussion from the rap on the head when you fell out of the ambulance."

"I jumped out," I explained. "I was escaping. I wasn't just sitting there, wringing my hands, waiting for the Queen's Messenger to arrive."

"The Queen's what?" asked Case. Then he waved his hand in an impatient gesture. "Never mind, just save it for the tape."

I was at the IGO installation for thirty-six hours in all. I told my story to a team of interrogators, a brace of tape recorders, and saw enough pictures of suspected agents to paper the walls of an average family home. If mug shots of unsavory types are your idea of smart decor, that is.

I was able to identify Dr. Kinsky, alias Professor Klein, alias goodness knows what else. He was a professional agent, working for the Dakaman insurgents, just as he'd said. He was one of those shadowy figures that the IGO knew about, but had no clear photos of. I spent a long time giving the interrogation team details on how he sat, moved, talked, and a whole raft of details I would have thought inconsequential. Especially in view of the fact that Dr. Kinsky was now undoubtedly a goner. No one could have survived that plunge from the bridge, and I'm sure the IGO dragged the Hudson River for days afterward.

The bright spot was that I got to see my Uncle Claude and my Aunt Lois, who didn't have to go back to Dakama after all. It seemed that after a bloody and vicious beginning, the would-be revolution was fast fizzling out. Mopping-up operations were in process in Dakama City even as we talked. Both were well, and in good spirits. Aunt Lois had her left arm in a sling. She'd had her shoulder fractured in the kidnap attempt. Being unable to write, she had inadvertently triggered the whole mess I'd become embroiled in. I'd spotted the handwriting as not hers. (It was Uncle Claude's. She'd dictated it.) It had set in motion the chain of events that led to my being kidnapped. And all because I'd suspected *she'd* been kidnapped!

I even found out how the IGO had known where to find me. It was the beeper in the shape of the *mezuzah*, the gadget Carl had said was useless! Well, to be fair, when I was being held in the hotel boiler room, it was. But once I was outside the hotel and in the street, and later, in the ambulance, the signal was picked up. It was luck that the men ordered to monitor the beeper frequently were still on the job at the time. No one had instructed them to shut down the receiver when I'd been "seen" at Kennedy Airport. While most of the IGO force was out at the airport, they picked up my signal. They called Case, who was directing operations from midtown New York. The rest, as they say, is history.

For good measure, the doping of the uniformed policeman didn't go unnoticed, either. It was seen by members of the crowd leaving the movie theater. When the cop's fellow officers came looking for him, the crowd told them what had happened. As the IGO was monitoring police frequencies, they picked that up, too. Which is how they knew they were looking for an ambulance at the bridge.

By the time I was driven back to my hotel, I felt that I'd been squeezed dry as a sponge. I also got a long session of dos and don'ts as to what I could safely discuss with anyone outside the IGO. If I obeyed all their instructions, I was virtually gagged. I wasn't looking forward to seeing Larry Small and Harry Grubb. They have that reporter's mentality. I had visions of fending off inquiries, but it didn't turn out that way.

When I got back to the Plaza, I'd expected to find the whole crew waiting for me. I was disappointed. They hadn't been told the exact time of my release from the IGO setup in New Jersey. So, when I checked for messages, I found a note saying that Carl was back on regular duty with the police, and if you can believe this, Harry Grubb and Larry Small were at a ball game at Yankee Stadium!

If that weren't enough, there was a cable from my

parents. They were currently en route to New York! They'd seen the TV reports about Dakama, and when they could reach neither me nor my aunt and uncle, they'd grabbed the first flight. They were due to arrive tomorrow. Swell. There went my vacation alone.

The note from Carl said that he'd be off duty by ten o'clock that evening and would meet me at Trader Vic's. The baseball game at Yankee Stadium was a twilight doubleheader, and wouldn't you know? They were all late. I consoled myself by Petunia-ing my way through a superb Polynesian dinner. Alone.

My "friends" arrived at Trader Vic's within ten minutes of each other. Larry and Harry Grubb were first. They were all questions, and I, by orders, was all evasions. Oddly enough, they respected my silence, once I'd explained that security forbade my discussing the facts in detail. But my big surprise came when Carl Suzuki arrived. Both Grubb and Larry Small greeted him like a long-lost brother!

It seems that, during my absence, the boys had become thicker than thieves. Larry had discovered something about Carl I didn't know. Carl had an extensive record collection of early 50's rock 'n' roll. Rhythm-and-Blues, actually. While the men ate a late dinner, the scintillating conversation was comprised of chitchat about Graig Nettles who, I understand, plays third base for the Yankees, and discussion on the comparative merits of vocal groups with names like *The Champs, The Chiffons, The Penguins,* and *The Bobbettes.*

Somehow, I managed to stay awake. Harry was his

usual acerbic self, and I must admit that he had more to say to me than my erstwhile suitors of three days past. I was beginning to think of myself as just one of the crowd. I must say that I'm all for ERA and equality, but they were going a bit too far. There are times when a woman doesn't want to be one of the other faces in the locker room. By the time dinner was ended, I was thoroughly miffed.

They even saw me to my suite as a group. I'd half expected that Larry and Carl would wait for an opportunity to see me alone. If only for some private talk. It was soon clear that wasn't about to happen. When they left me in my suite, they went off, arm in arm, still talking about music!

Then I figured it out. Each was waiting until he was alone. *Then* I'd get a telephone call. Sure. I watched a rerun of *Kojak,* part of the *Johnny Carson Show,* and was halfway through *Random Harvest* with Ronald Coleman on the Late Late Show before the phone rang. I flew across the room. But it was a long distance call. From California. The operator identified me, and said, "Go ahead, please."

"Hello? Doris?" came my mother's voice over the miles. "Are you all right? Your father and I have been worried sick!"

"I'm fine, Mommy," I assured her. "And you don't have to come to New York."

"I'm afraid it's too late for that," she said. "I'm calling from the airport. Your father and I will arrive in New York in . . . six hours. I'm not sure what time that will be there in the city. We've crossed so many time zones in the past few hours, I don't know my own name at this point."

"But Mommy," I protested, "it's not at all necessary. I'm well and happy. Aunt Lois and Uncle Claude will be back at their apartment soon. It's all right. Believe me!"

"I do, darling," my mother said. "But we have connecting flights. Even if we stayed here in California, our luggage would go to New York, anyway. Besides, we haven't been to New York since our honeymoon, your dad and I. It'll be fun!"

Sure it will, I thought. For *you*. I'll be here with the Hardy Boys, sitting like a lump while they talk. You and Dad will have a great time. And Doris goes back to being an overweight ornament. I said, "Swell, Mommy. Shall I try to reserve you a room?"

"It's not necessary, dear," my mother said. "We found a simply marvelous travel agent in Honolulu. He took care of it all. We'll be right with you, at the Plaza . . . Uh-oh. I think our flight is boarding now. Have to run, dear. See you soon!"

"Bye, Mommy," I said to the now dead phone. I went back to *Random Harvest*. I was beginning to feel like Greer Garson in that film. All through it, she has the hots for Ronald Coleman, but with one thing or another, they never get together until the last reel. And by then, they're so old it doesn't matter.

Next morning, my phone began to ring. My folks were downstairs in a room. Mommy was dying to see what the suites in the Plaza looked like. Larry Small called to say that he and Harry Grubb were leaving for Santa Amelia that afternoon. But still no call from Carl Suzuki. I told my folks that I'd meet them in the Palm Court for breakfast.

I'd cleaned up and was on my way past the desk in

135

the lobby to drop off my key. I'd turned and was headed for the Palm Court when the clerk called me back. "Letter for you, Ms. Fein," he said, pushing an envelope across the marble counter.

It had no stamp. Hand-delivered and typewritten. I opened it up and, if I'd expected a letter from Carl, I was again disappointed. It was from George Case.

Dear Ms. Fein:

Enclosed is your check for services rendered to the Organization. As you will note, it's a year's salary, at the figure we agreed upon. Please realize that you are on our payroll until this entire affair has been declassified by Security.

But note well that you are bound by cashing this draft to all the Internal Security procedures of the Organization. You are also subject to disciplinary measures for any breach of security. You will further advise us of any change in your address, telephone, and travel plans.

Sincerely,
G. T. Case
Director, IGO

I blinked at the amount of the check. A two, with four zeroes behind it. Things were looking up! As I walked through the lobby and toward the breakfast with my parents, thoughts began to buzz through my head.

I would give Larry and Carl another chance. I

would have a good time with my parents. And if neither of my ardent suitors made a move, and quickly, well . . . I had twenty thousand dollars, my passport, and the balance of my summer vacation. I've always wanted to see Paris.

About the Author

T. Ernesto Bethancourt, a native New Yorker of Puerto Rican descent, spent his early years in Brooklyn, New York and Tampa, Florida. He attended New York City public schools and the City University of New York. As Tom Paisley, he began a career as an entertainer when he was eleven years old, working as a child actor in radio. When he was older, he became a folk singer who was known not only for his blues and ballad singing, but as a writer of social satire in song. As Tom Paisley, he has written an off-Broadway musical and been a music critic and contributing editor for *High Fidelity* and *Hi-Fi Stereo Review* magazines. As T. Ernesto Bethancourt, he has written fourteen novels and several television film scripts.

Among his novels is *Doris Fein: Quartz Boyar,* also available from Vagabond Books.

He lives in Huntington Beach, California with his wife, Nancy, and their two daughters, Kimi and Thea.